STOLEN

Amazon Publishing
Attn: Amazon Children's Publishing
P.O. Box 400818
Las Vegas, NV 89140
www.amazon.com/amazonchildrenspublishing

[Library of Congress Cataloging-in-Publication Data

Vande Velde, Vivian.
Stolen / by Vivian Vande Velde. — 1st ed.
p. cm.
Summary: A girl finds herself running through the forest at the edge of a village with no memory of anything, even her own name, and later learns that she might be twelve-year-old Isabelle, believed to be stolen by a witch six years before.
ISBN 9781477816622
[1. Amnesia—Fiction. 2. Missing children—Fiction. 3. Witches—Fiction. 4. Family life—Fiction. 5. Magic—Fiction.] I. Title.
PZ7.V377Sto 2008
[Fic]--dc22
2008003184

Book design by Alex Ferrari
Editor: Margery Cuyler

First edition

PROLOGUE—THE OLD WITCH 7
1—THE BEGINNING 10
2—HERCULES TURNIP 17
3—COULD SHE BE A PRINCESS? 27
4—COULD SHE BE AN ANIMAL? 38
5—COULD SHE BE ISABELLE? 49
6—GOING HOME 57
7—AUNTIE ISABELLE 64
8—FAMILY 78
9—HOME SWEET HOME 89
10—BLOOD THICKER THAN WATER 101
11—ACCUSATIONS 110
12—THE WOODS 120
13—THE WITCH'S COTTAGE 126
14—DEEPER IN THE WOODS 131
15—MEMORIES 139
16—ISABELLE 142
17—ENDINGS AND BEGINNINGS 150

PROLOGUE

The old witch saw that she had gone too far. She had stolen one child too many, and the villagers had come after her.

She had thought there would be more time, time to pack those few things that were valuable to her and leave trouble behind. She had lived long enough that she had done this before.

And had lived long enough that there was no person she would regret leaving behind, no one who would mourn *her* absence.

But the angry villagers were already outside her cottage, banging on her door, shouting, demanding that she give herself and the baby up. Some of them had brought torches—she could smell the burning pitch—and there was only one reason for that in broad daylight.

Surely they wouldn't set fire to the cottage, the old witch hoped—not with the baby in here.

But sometimes, in a mob, there could be someone with

more temper than sense who would act without thinking, too quick for people with calmer heads to point out the grief that would result.

And always, where there's fire involved, there's the possibility of accidents.

The witch knew better than to try to talk her way out of this. They wouldn't listen. They would pretend to, agreeing to anything, until she handed over the baby.

The noise was frightening the baby. Or perhaps the infant sensed the old witch's fear. In any case, she was crying, her tiny face hot and flushed and wet with tears. Could the villagers hear her, above their own din? There was too big a chance that *someone* had, so it was no good simply to hide her away and try to convince everyone that they were mistaken, that the child had never been here.

There was a thud and a crunch of wood as something—a brawny shoulder or homemade battering ram—slammed into the witch's door. One of the boards bowed in from the pressure, but didn't snap.

Not this time.

But her cottage had not been built to withstand a mob.

She opened the shutters in the back of the house. Though she could see no villagers standing there, they still might be close enough to come running around from the front clearing, to grab her as soon as she crawled through the window. On the other hand, the side yards were crowded by the trees from the woods, so maybe none of the villagers had made their way back there. Yet.

Would leaving the baby behind gain her some time? Probably. First, the villagers might delay; and, even if not, the old witch could move faster without her.

But she was unwilling to give the child up.

The door shook on its hinges from a second blow, and the weak board splintered. The villagers' next try would bring the whole thing down.

The witch tucked the baby close, then squeezed through the window opening and jumped. They landed—harder than the witch would have thought from such a low height—on the ground beneath.

No villager was there to take hold of her, but that didn't mean she had escaped unseen.

The old witch ignored her aching bones. She didn't take the time to look over her shoulder to see if she was being pursued. Fear—and the baby's screams—made thinking difficult. She ran just until she was surrounded by trees. Then the old witch set the baby down on the forest floor.

And she cast the first of two hasty spells.

CHAPTER 1

The simplest way to begin is to start at the ending: The girl's name was Isabelle.

This is the simplest way because in the beginning she had no name—she was a girl with no name running through a forest she didn't know, for a reason she couldn't remember. She didn't know if she was running away from something or to something or for the simple joy of running.

At first, there was just the running, her feet slapping against the forest ground, right foot, left foot, right foot, left foot. She wasn't thinking. Her body was moving on its own, choosing—where there was no path—the clearest way, avoiding places where the roots stuck up out of the ground, breathing regularly so she wouldn't get a stitch in her side.

Then a piece of brush caught the hem of her dress, a moment no longer than an eyeblink of being held back—till, faster than thought, the fabric ripped and her momentum carried her forward again. Only then did the thought come: *I am running.*

And the next thought—several long moments later—was: *Why?*

She couldn't remember that anything or anyone was pursuing her; neither could she think of any place she needed to get to. And if she had started running for exuberance or enjoyment's sake, then the ripped hem and the ache that had started despite her measured breathing had ended the fun.

The girl who didn't know that her name was Isabelle stopped, resting her hand against her side.

Why am I running? she asked herself. And when she couldn't think what might be behind her or ahead of her, she tried to bring to mind what she remembered before becoming conscious of running.

No picture came to her.

None at all.

Neither where she was nor who she was.

And though, before, she had not been frightened, now she was.

What DO I know? she asked herself.

Obviously she knew how to run. She knew that running long and hard caused a pain in her side and that by breathing evenly she could delay the onset of that pain.

For the moment, her mind seemed blank beyond that.

How long have I been running?

She had no idea.

She looked around. She could tell she was in a forest, understood the concept of forest versus village, but she had in her head no names for a particular forest or any specific village. The leaves on the trees that surrounded her were a shade of green that she judged meant the season was early summer, and the quality of the light told her the hour wasn't yet noon.

Someone who could determine the season and the time of day should be able to fix upon what her own name was—but Isabelle could not.

Isabelle heard no sound beyond the faintest shivering of leaves in a gentle breeze. No sound of pursuit. But surely something was wrong, or she would know who and where she was. So she resumed running. But it wasn't as effortless as before. Her worry weighed her down as she tried to list the things she knew—and found the list of things she didn't know longer by far.

She was a girl about twelve summers old, she just *knew that* without having to think or look, without having to see her skirt around her legs or to feel her braids—loose and bedraggled—bouncing against her back. The glimpses she caught of stray sweaty wisps around her face showed she was dark haired. But whether plain or pretty, tanned or pale, she couldn't picture.

Stay calm, she told herself. *It will do you no good to panic.*

But that was easier said than done.

Her heart, already beating fast from running, was hammering madly in her chest. Her breathing was ragged, and she felt on the edge of tears.

Whatever has happened, she chided herself, *crying won't help*.

All right, so she was a dark-haired twelve-year-old girl. Did she have brothers or sisters? No faces drifted into her memory. But neither could she recall parents. Or foster parents. Not everyone has siblings, but everyone has some kind of parents. *Someone* must have raised her.

When still no faces came to her, she tried to make a joke of it: *What? Was I raised by wolves?* Which might have been funny if she had *known* it wasn't so.

She could picture wolves, but not a nurturing, child-rearing wolf. Besides, she reasoned, even the kindest-hearted wolf could not have provided her with clothing. She *must* have a family; she just couldn't remember them. Did *they* remember *her*? Had something awful happened to them? Was that why she was running?

Her pace had slowed as she tried to work things out, and now she stopped entirely, again pressing her hand to her side.

Once her mind stopped skittering in search of memories, and her heart stopped thudding so loudly, she found the forest was no longer quiet. She recognized the sound of yapping dogs in the not-too-distant distance.

I must be approaching a farm, she thought.

But the sound was getting louder, even though she had

stopped moving. So the dogs were approaching her. They were coming, she realized, from behind.

Isabelle had no memory of a reason to be afraid of dogs, so for several long moments she stood where she was, thinking she might follow the dogs after they passed her, thinking they might lead her to some human habitation.

But it was more than just one dog, or two—and suddenly she was afraid.

Dogs can't climb trees—that was one more thing Isabelle suddenly remembered. She didn't have any personal recollection of having climbed a tree, but she knew what to look for: low sturdy branches that gave access to higher sturdy branches.

None of the trees in her immediate area struck her as being especially good for climbing—especially in a dress—but the barking dogs were getting very near.

She grabbed hold of a branch that was at shoulder level. It sagged under her weight, which made hoisting herself up easier. But the branch's new downturn put her too low to reach the branch above. It was too far away for her to do more than graze her fingertips against its underside. She eased herself toward the trunk where her branch was thickest—and was still unable to grab the higher branch. The trunk was too smooth to get a foothold, and she was losing precious moments trying to make this tree work.

At least I'm off the ground, she told herself. But she knew she wasn't high enough: the dogs would be able to reach her.

Now! she commanded herself, guessing her nerve would fail her entirely once she could actually see the dogs.

She jumped to the ground and ran to another tree, one whose lowest branch was thick, but which required stretching to reach.

Just as her hands grasped the branch, the dogs—four of them—broke into the area where she was standing. Isabelle pulled herself up, raising her body off the ground, but her feet hung lower than when she'd been on the first tree. She was high enough to avoid a pack of rabid rabbits, but not these big snarly dogs with sharp teeth—dogs that were racing toward her as though she were the rabbit. Isabelle flung her legs upward.

But she didn't have enough momentum to get them high enough to go around the branch. Once more they dangled, like bait for the dogs.

She felt a tug on the skirt of her dress and realized one of the dogs had lunged and caught the trailing edge in its teeth. A mouthful of wool ripped away. Frantically, she swung her legs again, and this time was finally able to lock her ankles. Now she hung by her hands and her ankles up around the branch, like an oversized fruit about to drop from its own weight.

She could hear the nails of the dogs skritching against the bark of the trunk as the dogs leaped and snapped at her. One of them—she had no idea if it was the same dog as before—jumped off the ground and caught a corner of the now-ragged skirt. For a moment Isabelle's already straining hands and ankles supported the animal's weight as well as her own. Then the dog's teeth shredded through the fabric, and he fell free of her.

Isabelle's left leg was slipping, the bark scraping skin off her calf. She told herself to ignore the pain and tried to hold on, but her leg slid off the branch anyway and hung there, bare and defenseless. Unbalanced, her right foot began to slide, slowly, slowly.

The dog leaped at her skirt again, but by now the cloth was too tattered for him to hold on to it.

"Go away!" Isabelle screamed at the dogs.

The rough bark of the branch was cutting into her hands and scraping into her right ankle. She wasn't able to kick her left leg back up, and the other three dogs were now jumping, too. Though she was trying to keep her trailing leg as high as she could, one of the dogs grazed her with its claws.

Isabelle screamed again. No words this time, just pure, hopeless terror.

As her sweating hands were slipping and her body sagged lower yet, she thought she heard other yells besides her own, besides the baying of the dogs. But maybe not. Or, if someone *was* shouting at the dogs, calling them off—at least one of them did not obey. She felt its teeth sink into her leg, and the pain and the extra weight of the dog hanging from her own body was enough to loosen her grip entirely.

Isabelle fell to the ground, and blackness closed in on her.

CHAPTER 2

There was a throbbing pain in Isabelle's leg, but that was like an undercurrent she could ignore, more or less, by not allowing herself to awaken fully. But then Isabelle felt a cool, damp something-or-other touch below her ear, and that brought her back to the world.

Something had been wrong with her memory, she recalled, so that she had not been able to remember much. And then . . .

The dogs.

Them, she remembered. A pack of vicious dogs attacking her.

Just as she remembered, she heard a snuffling to accompany the cool, damp whatever-it-was that rubbed against her cheek, and she felt the brush of fur against her arm. She screamed and flung her arms out, sure the dogs were about to devour her.

As soon as her eyes focused, she saw she was no longer in the forest. Someone had laid her on a mattress by a fireplace, in a neat and clean little cottage, with golden afternoon sunshine streaming in through the open window.

There *was* a dog, but Isabelle knew immediately—well, almost immediately—it wasn't one of the ones that had attacked her, since it was on the smallish side, a light brown female whose belly hung low and lumpy. This dog was going to have pups, probably within a day or two.

Isabelle had obviously frightened the dog at least as much as the dog had frightened her, and it skittered into the corner and hung its head, clearly convinced that by nuzzling Isabelle it had done something wrong.

The front door flew open, and a man and a woman came running in. He was carrying a hoe, and she was wiping her hands on her apron.

Simple peasants, Isabelle thought, not sure where the thought had come from, since her memory had evidently not improved after being set upon by dogs and awakening dazed and confused.

"What happened?" the woman demanded. But she sounded worried, not annoyed or angry.

"She woke up," said a little girl's voice from the corner where the dog had retreated, and for a moment Isabelle wondered if the dog had spoken. The thought struck her as unusual, but not entirely impossible, yet she couldn't be sure if that was because of one of her forgotten experiences or from a story she had heard.

In any case a little girl stood up from the floor, a child of about six whom Isabelle had not noticed because the dog had been standing in front of her. The child said, "She woke up and scared Hercules Turnip."

The dog's tail thumped against the floor. Isabelle guessed that—despite the oddness of it—Hercules Turnip must be the animal's name.

"I'm sure Hercules Turnip scared *her*," the woman said, and smacked the man next to her on the arm, though he had said nothing.

"What?" he asked now.

All of this was somewhat reassuring, yet still disturbing. Someone had taken the trouble to rescue her from dogs that had seemed on the verge of tearing her apart. But who were her rescuers who had been kind enough to bring her into their own home and tend to her?

From some well of knowledge she didn't know she had, Isabelle pulled the impression that the couple—with their slightly bent backs and weathered faces—were too old to be parents to a six-year-old. Isabelle thought, *These must be the child's grandparents.*

The woman was glaring at the man significantly.

Clearly, the significance was lost on him just as much as it was lost on Isabelle. "What?" he repeated.

The woman spoke to him through clenched teeth, her lips hardly moving, as though this would direct her words only to him so that Isabelle couldn't hear—never mind that the room was of a size that nothing was much farther than four strides away from anything else. "See what you've done with those dreadful ill-trained dogs of yours? Now the poor thing has become fearful of all dogs, thinking they're all savage brutes."

"Hunter, Blackie, Spot, and Pointer are not savage brutes," the man protested. "They're good hunting d—"

The woman smacked his arm again, and he fell silent.

Isabelle felt it would be rude to take sides. Especially since it had been the man's voice she had heard—right before she had blacked out—calling the dogs off.

"Don't be afraid of *this* dog," the woman told Isabelle. "This is Hercules Turnip, and she's just a sweetheart that loves to mother all creatures."

Hercules Turnip's tail was in full wag now, for she plainly recognized her name and could tell she was being praised.

Though all of Isabelle's memory was of vicious dogs, she felt she could trust this one.

The little girl asked, "Can I come out of the corner now, Grandmother? I left her alone, just like you said. I never poked her, or played loud, or asked her questions, or did anything annoying at all. It was Hercules Turnip that woke her up, not me."

Sounding like someone who wasn't fooled easily, the woman said, "And I wonder how it was that Hercules Turnip came to wake her up?" To Isabelle, she said, "How's your poor leg feeling?" A rag had been tied around Isabelle's left leg, a much smaller rag than Isabelle would have expected, for she'd been sure the dogs in the forest had inflicted great gouges on her.

The leg had been aching when she woke up, but—between being startled by Hercules Turnip and trying to figure things out—Isabelle had somehow forgotten about it. She admitted, "It doesn't hurt too terribly much."

The woman sat on the edge of the mattress and undid the bandage.

Isabelle forced herself to look, ready to avert her eyes if the wound was too ghastly. She half expected that the cloth, despite its small size, was all that was keeping her leg from falling off, so she was pleasantly surprised to see only red angry-looking punctures from the dog's teeth—but no flesh missing, no bones broken. It was the spot above the bite, where the tree's bark had scraped off the top layer of skin, that hurt the most.

"Will she live, Grandmother?" the little girl asked, coming closer.

"Hush, Ravyn," the woman said. "Of course she'll live. There was never any doubt of that."

But this woman had never been clinging to a tree branch, snarling dogs below her, dogs that clearly wanted to feast on her. *Oh yes, there WAS a doubt*, Isabelle thought.

The little girl—Ravyn, apparently—also was not convinced. "Orsen says you can never be sure," she said. "Orsen says sometimes even a little wound goes bad, sometimes even a little wound on your little finger that doesn't look like anything; but it festers, and the bad blood creeps up into your hand so they need to chop off your finger, and then it creeps from your hand up your arm so they need to—"

"Ravyn!" The woman turned back to Isabelle. "I have seen dog bites before, and this is not as bad as I'm sure it feels. The cloth has been soaked in chamomile, and here is some more crushed yarrow to keep the wounds from getting inflamed."

In fact, Isabelle recognized the herbs' smells, though she didn't know from where. "Thank you," she said, for the reassurance, and for the care she had clearly been given. *Do I know you?* she wondered. Had these people rescued her and brought her into their home and bound her wounds and placed her by the warmth of the fire because they were her family?

She was about to ask when the woman, smiling kindly, said, "Your kin must be worried about you. Tell us who they are, and we will send them word."

Oh.

Slowly, Isabelle said, "I don't know. I don't know my name."

The woman reached backward to smack her husband's arm again.

He had apparently learned that it did no good to ask why, but had *not* learned to move out of her range.

"That's strange," the woman said. "The dogs must have frightened your name right out of you. It will come back in a moment. Meanwhile, I'll tell you my name. It's Avis, and this is Browley, and this is our granddaughter, Ravyn."

Ravyn said, "And this is Hercules Turnip."

With no name to contribute to the conversation, Isabelle asked, "Why?"

"*Hercules* because she's strong. When I was little more than a baby and she was just a puppy, I fell into the creek, and she pulled me out and kept me from drowning to death. And *Turnip* because of her color," said Ravyn.

Another memory—another of those insignificant memories that did nothing to help her—fell into place in Isabelle's head. "I thought Hercules was a boy's name."

Ravyn said, "Then why does it start with *Her*?"

Having no answer, Isabelle said, "Well, maybe you're right."

Ravyn nodded as though she were used to being right.

"And *your* name?" Avis prodded gently.

The delay hadn't helped. "I don't know," Isabelle said again.

Avis turned to Browley. "See? Those dogs of yours frightened her so badly she can't even remember her name."

"I'm sorry," Browley said to Isabelle. "When I saw they'd treed a little slip of a girl, and them baying at the tree, and you about to fall, I called them off. But Hunter didn't hear right off. He's not a *bad* dog. . . ."

"No," Isabelle told them, "it wasn't the dogs. I couldn't remember my name even before."

The family all looked at one another, distressed. Even

Hercules Turnip cocked her head and wore a thoughtful expression.

"You couldn't remember . . .?" Avis started.

". . . anything," Isabelle finished.

Browley whistled.

They were all silent, clearly with no idea what to say. And that was scary.

Finally Ravyn said, "The old witch of the forest must have put a curse on her."

Isabelle had a quick mental image of an old woman in the kitchen of a cottage even smaller than this one. Isabelle felt afraid, but couldn't remember of what.

Avis tried to smack Ravyn's arm, but the child could move quickly. "No," Avis said to Ravyn.

Her voice burst the picture in Isabelle's head like a bubble.

And to Isabelle, Avis said, "Most likely it was the dogs. You just got confused about when you lost your memory because of how frightened and hurt you've been."

That must be it, Isabelle thought. But she knew it wasn't.

Avis was telling her, "Don't you worry your head. We'll find out your name, and once we do and you hear it, everything will come back to you."

That was a hope to hold on to.

"Is it Ravyn?" Ravyn asked. And when Isabelle shook her head, Ravyn asked, "Is it Dena, or Summer, or Erwina?"

"Ravyn," Avis said. "We know all those girls. They're all your friends."

"She could have the same name as one of my friends," Ravyn pointed out. "Is it Willa—"

"Ravyn, enough! The poor girl is tired from her ordeal, and you're making her more tired."

"I'm just being helpful," Ravyn protested.

Isabelle was getting light-headed again, and her leg was beginning to throb. She wanted to lie down, to close her eyes. "Thank you for all your kindness," she said, and was surprised to hear how weak and quavery her voice sounded.

"Oh hush!" Avis gave her a hug. "You just rest now, girl. Things will be better the next time you wake up."

Isabelle watched Avis stand up. She heard the clump of Browley's boots as he walked outside to finish whatever work her scream had called him indoors from, and she heard the outside dogs—Browley's hunting dogs that had attacked her—bark to greet him. Her stomach tightened at their noise. She heard Ravyn ask, "Can I give her a name?"

Her grandmother answered, "The girl *has* a name, even if we don't know it yet."

"But what if she doesn't remember soon? What if she never remembers?"

These were Isabelle's fears, too, though her mind was beginning to shut down and drift away as sleep approached.

Ravyn said, "I can think up just the right name for her.

I'm good at thinking up names. Hercules Turnip *loves* her name."

"The wrong name will be more confusing to her than no name at all," said Avis.

"Hmph!" Ravyn said. Then, before Isabelle drifted off entirely, she heard Ravyn say, "And I bet it *was* the old witch who took away her memory."

CHAPTER 3

Isabelle awoke to the smell of cooking. With her eyes still closed, she knew it was stew; she could pick out the scents of carrots and peas and onions, a bit of rosemary, possibly parsley, and there was meat which she was fairly certain was duck, though it might be goose. Earlier, the day being warm, the fire in the fireplace had been little more than embers, kept alive so that a whole new fire didn't need to be kindled for cooking meals. But now Isabelle could hear the flames snapping, and she could feel the warmth on her legs even though there was no weight of a blanket on her, so that she knew she must have kicked the blanket off in her sleep. Though no one was speaking, she could hear the family in the room: a slow, heavy step that must be Browley's; Avis moving methodically around the table, setting out wooden bowls; Ravyn skipping back and forth with her usual excess energy; Hercules Turnip trying to keep up with Ravyn.

Isabelle knew all this. But she still didn't know her name.

"You're awake!" Ravyn cried the moment Isabelle's eyes opened, and she hurled herself onto the mattress. Though she didn't land on Isabelle's leg, she jostled it, sending sharp pains from Isabelle's calf through her thigh, up her back, and to her head, so that it felt as if someone had cracked her on the forehead with a board.

"Sorry," Ravyn said. The dizzying pain cost Isabelle a moment or two, and she wasn't sure if she had cried out or if Ravyn could tell by her face what had happened. "Sorry."

"Honestly, child," Browley muttered, lifting Ravyn up off the mattress, "if you don't calm down, we'll put you out with the chickens."

"No, no," Ravyn squealed, but she was laughing—obviously this was an old joke between them—"not with the chickens!"

"For goodness' sakes," Avis grumbled. "I'll put you both out. Neither one of you is fit to live in a house like civilized people." She rested her hand against Isabelle's forehead. The hand was chapped and rough, but the touch was gentle.

Isabelle couldn't be sure, but she had the impression it had been a very long time since someone had felt her forehead to determine if she had a fever.

"Feeling better? Except for the damage inflicted by the wild holligan? The wild hooligan *somebody* was supposed to be watching?"

"Yes," Isabelle said, because the touch itself—the concern behind it—was comforting, but she had to close her eyes against the nausea that set the room spinning around her.

Isabelle heard a low whine and felt Hercules Turnip lick her hand.

"See," Ravyn said, "*everyone* wants you to feel better."

"I do," Isabelle insisted. She managed to sit up, and after a moment the room stopped moving.

Avis looked deep into her eyes—and Isabelle suspected she knew, even before Browley asked, "Anything come back to you?"

"Not yet," Isabelle admitted.

"Maybe after a good meal," Browley said.

Maybe after a rest, maybe after a meal. Maybe never. *What if she never remembers?* Ravyn's words echoed in Isabelle's head.

Would I still be me, Isabelle wondered—*whoever me is*—*if I don't ever remember?*

Avis gave her a reassuring hug: firm, but mindful of Isabelle's injuries. Then she wet a cloth for Isabelle to wash her hands and face with.

Isabelle also cleaned her leg, above the bandage, where the bark of the tree had rubbed her raw. These wounds were already scabbed over and beginning to itch, which was probably a good sign.

Avis told her, "If you need to, you can have your meal a'bed. But it would probably be better for you to come to the table, so your leg doesn't stiffen."

It already had. Still, Isabelle managed to hobble to the

table, and the stew was tasty.

Avis and Browley asked her all manner of questions to try to uncover her lost memories: Did she live on a farm or in a town? What did her father do to keep the family fed? Did he till the earth, as Browley did? Or did he work with metal, or with wood, or straw, or leather, or stone? Did he tend rich men's horses? Did she have any memory of animals: sheep or goats or fish? Was her home wattle or wood or stone? Did her mother cook for other people, or just for the family?

Isabelle recognized all the words and concepts, but could form no clear picture of herself in any of the situations the old couple described for her.

Ravyn's questions were no more helpful: What were her chores around the house? Was her best friend a boy or a girl? Had she ever seen a unicorn or a griffin or a sea monster? What was her favorite color? Which was her favorite flower? Whose song did she think was prettier—a goldfinch's or a greenfinch's?

After the meal was over and cleaned up, and they were no closer to discovering who Isabelle was than when she had first awakened, Ravyn said, "Well, I think she's a princess who has had a magical spell put on her, and that's why she can't remember anything."

A princess. Isabelle tried that possibility out in her head. Living in a palace, wearing beautiful gowns, having people wait on her. All of that would be pleasant, Isabelle mused, but she suspected it was improbable.

Avis rolled her eyes and fetched the basket where she kept the raw wool and spindle for drawing out yarn.

Isabelle noted that she knew what the objects were—basket, wool, yarn, and spindle—but none of this offered any insight into her previous life, either.

"A princess is not so very likely," Browley was telling Ravyn. "Princesses are in short supply in this corner of the countryside."

Ravyn refused to be put off so easily. "She could be." Then she added, "Look how soft and clean her skin is. And her hair."

Isabelle didn't feel clean, after running in the woods, and climbing a tree, and falling out of that tree into a pack of dogs. Ravyn was a bit grimy, and her hair was tangled, but wasn't that typical of young children?

Isabelle looked at her hands, which were definitely softer than Avis's, and had no scars or calluses.

Ravyn stood up abruptly, causing her stool to scrape against the floor and tip over. "Are you used to people doing this to you?" she asked. She flourished her hand with as much grace as though a honeybee was near her face, and gave an exaggerated bow. In a solemn voice, she said, "Your wish is my command, your royal highness."

Isabelle couldn't help but laugh.

Her injured leg made standing difficult, so she returned the bow from her seat and admitted, "No, I think I can be fairly certain no one has ever said that to me before."

Not discouraged, Ravyn insisted to her grandparents, "I bet she is. I bet she's a princess, and the old witch who lives in the forest stole her away."

Again, the picture came into Isabelle's head of the old woman. She wasn't a-little-bit old like Avis; she was as old as dirt. Where had that thought come from? In Isabelle's head, a little girl's voice chanted:

Old as dirt,
dirty as dirt.
Ugly as sin,
mean as sin.
Don't let the old witch catch you!

Nasty little girl, Isabelle thought.

Then she wondered: *Is that me?*

Had she been spiteful enough—and foolish enough—to taunt an old woman who may or may not have been a witch? Because, the fact that this woman's face floated at the edges of Isabelle's memory every time someone said the word *witch* suggested that maybe Isabelle had once seen a witch after all.

Could a witch, taunted beyond endurance, have bespelled her?

All the while Isabelle was worrying about witches—and the kind of girl she might have been—*this* family was still talking about princesses.

Avis said, "That isn't the kind of dress a princess would wear, Ravyn."

Ravyn said, "It probably wasn't ripped until the dogs chased her."

"Princesses are clothed in satins and silks," Avis told her, "not wools and linens."

Wearing a superior expression, Ravyn said, "When the old witch stole her from her castle, she took her nice dress away and made her wear this one."

Without answering, Avis tossed the spindle to Isabelle.

Isabelle caught it. And once she held it, her hands instinctively knew what to do, her left hand pinching the fibers, her right twisting the spindle and letting it drop, so that the wool was drawn out and wrapped itself around the spindle.

Not, Isabelle thought, *a skill a princess is likely to find necessary to her daily royal life.*

Avis didn't bother to point this out.

Ravyn was not distracted. "And the old witch forced her to work," she finished. "That's why she stole her away to begin with."

Though that didn't fit in with the smooth hands.

"*Is* there an old witch in the forest?" Isabelle asked.

"Yes," Ravyn said.

"No," Avis said.

"Not anymore," Browley said.

Avis smacked his arm.

"If there ever was one," Browley amended.

Isabelle waited, and Avis explained, "There was an old woman—a solitary old soul—who some of the villagers went to for potions and remedies."

Isabelle again saw the old woman in her kitchen, tying up bundles of dried herbs.

"And curses," Ravyn added knowingly.

"Perhaps," Avis said. "Sometimes, when things went right, people said it was because of something they had bought from the old woman. And sometimes, when things went wrong, people suspected the old woman had sold something of a different nature to a foe or a rival. Finally people decided they'd had enough of her so-called wicked ways, and they burned her house down—with her in it."

"Unless," Ravyn finished, "she escaped. Witches are tricky."

No memories came, only a twisting feeling in Isabelle's stomach. "It sounds as though the wicked ones were the ones who went to her asking for a curse."

"Perhaps," Avis said again.

"But who would have put a curse on you?" Ravyn asked. "Or did the witch steal you away from your home, forcing you to work for her and stealing away your memories, just because that was something *she* wanted to do?"

Once again the childish jeer played through Isabelle's mind:

Old as dirt,
dirty as dirt.
Ugly as sin,
mean as sin.
Don't let the old witch catch you!

"We don't know that's what happened," both Isabelle and Avis said, speaking at the same time.

Ravyn looked down her nose at the two of them and asked, "Then why else did you show up in the forest on the very day the old witch died—or fled away? The old witch *liked* to steal children. She—"

"Ravyn," Avis chided, "don't put scary thoughts into the poor girl's head. She's been through enough without worrying about such nonsense as magic and witches."

Isabelle rummaged around in her own head to see if she believed in witchcraft—not in stories, but in real life.

Yes, she thought she did.

But Ravyn's grandmother was such a wise and capable person, it was hard not to suspect that Avis's conviction was truer than Ravyn's belief and Isabelle's own newly found suspicion that there was such a thing as witches in the world.

Isabelle had so much to relearn.

She learned something new that night, when Ravyn had gone to bed in her corner of the room, and Browley and Avis in theirs, and Isabelle was resting on her mattress by the fireplace.

The fire had been banked for the night so that the embers could be recalled to life in the morning, but meanwhile the only light came from the candle by Avis and Browley's bed. Then Browley blew out that last candle.

And Isabelle learned she was afraid of the dark.

She sat up so abruptly that Ravyn called over, "What's wrong?"

"Nothing," Isabelle said. Ravyn was five or six years younger, and *she* obviously wasn't afraid of the dark.

Isabelle lay back down and tried to tell herself that all was safe in the little cottage, that there was nothing to fear in the shadows that loomed in the corners, the shadows that pressed in on her and made it hard for her to breathe.

"Girl?" Avis asked.

And Isabelle realized she had been breathing so hard, they all must have heard. "Good night," she said for a second time.

It was Browley who guessed. "Does the dark disturb you?"

There's nothing there, Isabelle tried to tell herself. But in a small voice she admitted, "Yes."

Ravyn said, "We can light a candle for you."

"Danger of fire," Avis pointed out. "Browley, open the shutter a crack for the moonlight to get in."

Browley did, though Avis warned, "Not so much, or we'll all catch a chill."

"Better?" Browley asked Isabelle.

"Yes," she said, though it wasn't *much* better.

"See?" Ravyn said. "She's a princess, who's used to hundreds of bright candles in every room."

Avis said, "Which would still need to be extinguished at night for the danger of fire."

Undeterred, Ravyn said, "And then the old witch locked her up in the dark old cellar."

"*Good night*, grandchild."

Isabelle lay in the almost-dark, her mind skittering from one thing to another, wondering who she was and trying to determine how she could find out what had happened to her. Afraid of the dark, afraid that she didn't know enough to know what she should be afraid of—she felt that her heart was sure to burst in her chest from the strain. Repeatedly, she tried to empty her mind of questions and plans, and wished for sleep—or morning—to come.

CHAPTER 4

The morning dawned with no new insight as to who Isabelle could be.

Browley was of the opinion that Isabelle still couldn't remember anything because she had slept restlessly, and he was convinced *this* was due to the ache in her leg.

"As her wound heals," he maintained, "she will sleep better. And once she sleeps well, her memory is sure to return."

Isabelle thought Avis and Ravyn looked skeptical. Isabelle was skeptical, but because of his kindness, she tried not to let her doubts show on her face.

In truth, her leg was much less sore than it had been. Avis's herbs were working. Isabelle was able to get out of bed without much pain, and she found she could help a bit in the kitchen, if she moved slowly. She also found that she knew how to bake bread, which was a puzzle to Ravyn—who declared a princess shouldn't know kitchen work unless forced to do it by a witch—and a relief to Avis, who was now freed up to help Browley in the field.

As soon as her grandmother left, Ravyn began to try out various names on Isabelle: Princess Alvina, Princess Elbertine, Princess Daisy.

None struck Isabelle as a good fit.

Perhaps the first step to learning about her own past was to learn about the past of this family who had taken her in, and about the village in which they lived. So Isabelle asked, "Tell me about this witch your grandparents don't believe in."

"It's Grandmother who doesn't believe," Ravyn said. "Grandfather does. Grandfather helped hunt her down."

A cold chill crept up Isabelle's back. Sweet, kind Browley?

And his hunting dogs.

It was one thing to have them hunt game and the occasional stray memory-less girl. But to hunt down an old woman who may or may not have been a witch . . .

"Well then," Isabelle said, forcing her voice not to show anything, "tell me about that."

In a voice of delicious horror, Ravyn said, "The witch steals children away."

Isabelle realized she knew this already; Ravyn had hinted at something of the sort last night. "You mean *wicked* children?" A piece of memory had fallen into place in Isabelle's mind: Sometimes parents threatened children to behave or . . . *something* would get them—the fairies, the goblins, the bedbugs. Maybe around here it was the old witch of the forest.

But Ravyn was shaking her head. "Any child. Sometimes even a baby. This last time it was Mady's baby. Her teeny, tiny baby who couldn't have done anything wrong. She was only a month old." Just in case Isabelle was unfamiliar with babies, Ravyn added, "Babies who are only a month old don't do much of anything, good or wicked. She didn't even have a name yet. Mady and Frayne were waiting for Brother Ainsley to come from the monastery to baptize her. The baby was born just after Brother Ainsley left last time. I only saw her once. Honey—that's Mady's older daughter—she let me look while her mother was sleeping, and Honey said I could hold her if I brought a bucket of berries for her—for Honey, not the baby—and I wasn't to tell Mady because they were to be *just* for Honey. Honey is almost eighteen and kind of fat and very lazy. But, before I had a chance to hold the baby, the old witch stole her away."

"Why?" Isabelle asked. Babies are a lot of work—that was something else she knew without knowing how. Why would an old witch want more work? It was one thing for this witch to have stolen away Isabelle, if that was what had happened, since a twelve-year-old could be put to work doing chores.

Ravyn shrugged. "I don't know. Orsen thinks she eats them. She stole away other children, too, but not while anybody was looking. People thought it was her, but they couldn't be sure. She stole another of Honey's sisters a long time ago, near when I was born. That one was six. But this time Honey saw and she screamed for help, and people went after the witch. Grandfather, too. But because we live on the other side of the village, he didn't hear about it right away, and he didn't get there until after the old witch's house was already burning."

"Did they really burn the house?" Isabelle asked in horror. "With the baby in there?"

Ravyn shook her head. "The baby was gone. So was the old witch. I know that's true. Nobody's seen either one of them. Only, Orsen says they shouldn't have burned the house down. Orsen says the old witch probably used her magic to disguise herself and the baby to look like ordinary things like a spoon or a rug or a stool or something, so nobody would know it was them. Orsen says they probably both went up in the fire. But I think sometimes Orsen doesn't know what he's talking about."

Isabelle hoped so, too.

Besides, if the witch *had* cast a spell on her, then the witch might well be the only one in the world who knew who she was.

A witch who steals babies is scary, Isabelle thought.

But maybe not as scary as never finding out who I am.

Unless, of course, finding out who she was turned out to be worse than not knowing.

Maybe, a little voice nagged at her, *there's a good reason you forgot.*

Still, Isabelle was determined that as soon as her leg was better, she would go out into the world and ask about herself and ask about the witch and ask about whatever she needed to ask about—until she had some answers.

But before that, and shortly before the adults were due back for the midday meal, Hercules Turnip became restless, drank a lot of water, then lay on her side and started panting.

"It's the puppies!" Ravyn cried. "What should we do? I'll get Grandmother—no, Grandfather—no, Grandmother. I'll get them both. Will she be all right? Orsen says lots of times a dog loses her first litter, so I should prepare myself for the worst. You don't think Hercules Turnip is going to lose her litter, do you? That doesn't happen if a dog is strong, does it? You watch her while I get Grandmother and Grandfather."

Isabelle assured her, "Hercules Turnip knows what to do. She'll be fine. You don't need to get your grandparents." Her own certainty made her suspect that in her former life she had seen enough animals giving birth so as not to find this an occasion for panic.

That seemed yet another indication she probably wasn't a princess: princesses were well known to be delicate and dainty.

Looking unconvinced, Ravyn demanded shrilly, "What should I do to help?"

"Speak softly," Isabelle suggested, for the sake of her own ears as much as for Hercules Turnip's. "Reassure her that she's doing fine and that all will be well."

Sometime between the second and third puppies, Avis and Browley returned for the meal Isabelle had prepared and set out. Under Ravyn's direction, they offered effusive praise and encouragement to Hercules Turnip. Ravyn did pull them aside, however, to offer quietly—for her—the opinion that, even though the puppies were very cute, they were also quite slimy and a bit disgusting. "Don't tell Hercules Turnip," Ravyn instructed as they prepared to go back out into the fields. "We don't want to hurt her feelings."

Hercules Turnip gave birth to five squirmy pups, which Isabelle felt was a fine number for a first litter. "Well done, Hercules Turnip," she said, and the new mother panted happily from the corner she had selected near the fireplace and the foot of Isabelle's mattress.

In the middle of the afternoon, just as Ravyn was showing signs of growing bored with the puppies since they couldn't be handled yet, there was a visitor.

"Orsen!" Ravyn cried when the boy appeared on their doorstep. "Hercules Turnip had her puppies! I helped! Want to see?"

Orsen was slightly younger than Ravyn, a stocky little boy with light-colored hair and a bit of a know-it-all expression made bearable only because it was accompanied by a sweet smile.

Fortunately, Hercules Turnip was of a calm disposition and allowed the children to come close.

"Only five?" Orsen asked. "My dog had seven pups." Then he added, "That one looks like a runt. That's too bad. Runts die."

"It's not a runt," Ravyn protested. "Is it, Princess . . ." She was obviously too distressed to think of a new name at this time, so just repeated, "Princess?"

"No," Isabelle assured her, "just small."

"Princess Princess?" Orsen said. "What kind of name is that?"

"Temporary," Isabelle told him. She was ready to take back the opinion that his smile was sweet.

But just then he smiled again. "You're the lost girl Ravyn's grandfather found. He told my father you don't know who you are. Is that true? You don't know who you are?"

"No, I don't," Isabelle admitted.

"Even my baby brother knows who he is," Orsen said, "and he was only born on the Feast of the Magi. But if you call out 'Derwin,' he kicks his legs and smiles. Father says it's gas, but Mother says he knows his name."

"That's nice," Isabelle said.

Ravyn told Orsen, "She knows her name; she just forgot it because the old witch of the forest put a spell on her."

"Did she?" Orsen asked Isabelle.

"If so," Isabelle told him, "I forgot."

"That's too bad," Orsen said. "Why does Ravyn call you Princess Princess?"

Ravyn said, "Because she's a princess."

"You remember being a princess?" Orsen asked.

"No," Isabelle said.

"But she is one, all the same," Ravyn said. "Look at her hands. They're so smooth and white."

Embarrassed, Isabelle held her hands out for Orsen to see.

"I don't think she's a princess," Orsen said.

"I don't think I'm a princess, either," Isabelle agreed.

"Why not?" Ravyn asked Orsen.

He shook his head.

"Why not?" Ravyn insisted.

Orsen leaned in closer to her, but his whisper carried: "Princesses are supposed to be pretty."

"She's sort of pretty," Ravyn said out loud, which would have given Orsen away even if Isabelle hadn't overheard him.

Still whispering, Orsen said, "Not pretty enough."

Ravyn looked at Isabelle and didn't say anything to defend her—which shouldn't have stung, but did.

Ravyn said, "Well, if she's not a princess, why did the old witch put a spell on her to make her forget who she is?"

Orsen looked Isabelle over. "I think," he said, "she isn't even human at all."

"Now, see here . . ." Isabelle put her hand on her hip.

This time Ravyn *did* come to her defense. "She might not be pretty enough to be a princess, but she isn't animal-ugly."

Isabelle crossed her arms over her chest. "No, no. You're too kind," she said. "All this flattery will go to my head."

Orsen insisted, "No, it has to be: The old witch wouldn't *just find* a princess in the forest. She took an animal, and cast a spell to turn it into a girl." Seeing Isabelle's scowl, he tried to soften that by adding, ". . . a . . . sort-of . . . pretty girl."

"Do you remember being an animal?" Ravyn asked.

"No," Isabelle snapped. But then she thought about it. *Could* Orsen be right? Her first memories were of running in the forest, and she had absolutely no recollection of being with people before Avis and Browley and Ravyn had taken her in.

Orsen asked Ravyn, "Have you noticed her doing things like an animal? Like scratching her neck with her foot? Or baying at the moon?"

"She eats like a person," Ravyn said, but hesitantly.

"Isn't it time for you to go home?" Isabelle asked Orsen.

"I'm only trying to help," he told her. "It might explain why Ravyn's grandfather's dogs chased you. Usually, they help him catch ducks and geese. Maybe, even though you look like a person to us, you smelled like an animal to them."

Isabelle saw their noses discreetly sniff the air.

Orsen said, "Well, dogs' noses can smell more things than people's noses can. Do you find yourself flapping your arms and trying to fly?"

"No," Isabelle said. "And I don't seem to smell like an animal to Hercules Turnip."

Ravyn said, "Hercules Turnip loves everyone and everything.

She rescued a baby rabbit that was being chased by a badger last summer. She brought the baby rabbit to us to take care of until he was grown enough to be on his own. I named him Merton Flop-Ear: *Flop-Ear* because his one ear was floppy, *Merton* after my friend Summer's father who died when he wasn't fast enough to outrun a bear."

Ravyn was starting to make Isabelle feel light-headed.

"Could you be a rabbit?" Orsen asked.

"No," Isabelle said again. "When I was being chased by the dogs, I climbed a tree, and a rabbit would never think to do that. And I never thought about flying away, so I'm not a bird." She *couldn't* be an animal. She felt like a person. Didn't she? Just . . . a person with no memory. Surely an animal didn't feel like this?

Orsen said, "And since you're not flopping on the ground unable to breathe, you're probably not a fish. How about a squirrel? Do you like nuts?"

Isabelle's eyes were beginning to sting. "I am not an animal," she said.

"No," Ravyn said softly. "But maybe an animal-turned-into-a-person?"

"Do things look smaller to you than you're used to?" Orsen asked. "Like you're used to being the size of a bear? Or do things look big, like you're used to being a chipmunk?"

"Neither," Isabelle insisted. "I'm just the right size."

"Maybe," Orsen said, "you just can't remember being a different size."

"You're making her angry," Ravyn said, and Isabelle realized Ravyn was right. *Isabelle* had thought she was just getting sad, but now she realized she was angry, too. What kind of person doesn't even know if she's sad or angry? Wasn't that more like an animal than a person?

"Do you want to bite me?" Orsen asked.

Actually, that *was* a tempting idea, but Isabelle fought the impulse.

Then the door burst open, and a woman walked in—her cheeks streaked with tears. Was it Orsen's mother? Had Orsen's mother come to rescue him from the animal that thought it was a girl?

But the woman didn't look at Orsen or Ravyn, only at Isabelle.

Then the woman burst into sobs, held her arms out, and cried, "Isabelle!"

CHAPTER 5

This woman thinks she knows me, Isabelle said to herself as the woman flung her arms about her and rocked her from side to side.

She didn't look at all familiar to Isabelle.

If I mean enough to her that she's weeping to see me here safe, shouldn't SOMETHING be stirring in my heart when I look at her?

Nothing stirred.

Ravyn sidled up to Isabelle and said, in one of her probably-meant-to-be-a-whisper voices, "That's Mady."

Mady. The woman who had lost two children to the old witch: a month-old baby yesterday and an older daughter six years ago, about the time Ravyn had been born. A daughter who—if she were still alive—would now be Isabelle's age.

She thinks I'm her long-lost daughter Isabelle.

Isabelle.

The name seemed neither familiar nor alien.

Can I be?

Surely a mother should recognize her own child.

But shouldn't—just as surely—a child recognize her own mother?

She was aware of Ravyn's friend Orsen watching her, no doubt weighing her reactions against how an animal might behave.

Mady had her cheek pressed against Isabelle's. Her skin was hot and damp and splotched with red, her eyes were bloodshot from all her crying, and her entire body heaved with emotion as she waited for Isabelle to return her hug.

All Isabelle needed was to lift her arms.

Admittedly, this would be slightly awkward since Mady's embrace had Isabelle's arms more or less pinned to her sides, but it was the right thing to do, for a daughter to warmly acknowledge her tearful mother whom she had not seen in so many years.

Beyond the crying woman, beyond Ravyn and Orsen nudging each other as they waited for Isabelle to do *something*, Isabelle saw Avis in the open doorway of the cottage, wiping her hands on her apron, also watching her.

I am being coldhearted, Isabelle thought. *The woman who is probably my mother—my mother who never thought to see me again—is standing here with her heart breaking for joy, and I am noticing how crying has made her nose run and her skin blotch.*

And then Isabelle thought, *What did the witch do to me, to leave me so unfeeling, so uncaring?*

Avis was still watching her—Avis, who was no relation to her at all, but who had been generous with her hugs, her comforting.

For Avis's sake—so as not to appear a terrible person in her eyes—Isabelle pulled one arm free. Awkwardly, self-consciously, feeling a fraud, she patted Mady's back.

Ravyn had said Mady's child had been six years old when she was taken.

Isabelle thought, *There's a big difference between a six-year-old and a twelve-year-old.*

Was Mady just guessing, hoping?

But if so, Isabelle's hesitant and ungraceful hug had obviously convinced her.

"Oh, Isabelle!" Mady said, then gasped, sounding as though the effort of trying to speak on top of all that sobbing was going to make her gag and vomit. "Oh, Isabelle."

Isabelle cringed, tensed, ready to move quickly out of the way should that be necessary, even as she recognized that squeamishness was not the emotion this situation called for.

Avis had come into the room, gesturing at Ravyn and Orsen to step back, though they shuffled their feet more than they moved away. Now Avis fetched a ladle full of water, having to step carefully over Hercules Turnip and the puppies. She held the ladle out to Mady. "Mady," she said, "calm yourself. Why don't you sit?"

But Mady ignored both Avis and the water. "Have you seen your little sister?" she asked.

Isabelle glanced at Ravyn before she remembered that Ravyn *wasn't* her little sister—there wasn't any question at all about that. Shrill, annoying, noisy, nosy Ravyn: it was the first time Isabelle realized she felt sisterly toward her.

Ever helpful, Ravyn said in her loud whisper, "She means the baby—the one the witch took yesterday."

Not to be outdone, Orsen asked, "Did you see what the witch did to her? Did she change her into something, like a broom, or a doorstop, or a pot pie, or—ow!" Apparently Orsen wasn't as experienced at ducking Avis's smacks to the arm as Ravyn was. "That hurt," Orsen said solemnly, though Isabelle doubted it did, not from the distance Avis had needed to stretch across to reach him. But that didn't stop him from rubbing his arm dramatically, as though he had lost all feeling in the limb.

"The girl remembers nothing," Avis told Mady.

Orsen started, "Well, that's probably because—"

Avis clapped her hand over his mouth.

I should be delighted that someone is laying claim to me, Isabelle thought. This was what she had hoped for. But she had assumed that—once it happened—her memories would come rushing back to her, that she wouldn't need any explanations but would remember everything.

That she would no longer have any doubts.

Avis asked Mady, "Are you sure she's Isabelle? Wasn't Isabelle's hair lighter and straighter?"

"So was Honey's," Mady said, "when *she* was a little tot."

A voice from the doorway said, "My hair wasn't *that* much lighter than it is now. That's why everyone has always called me Honey, because of the color of my hair. And it's still honey colored, besides being naturally curly."

Isabelle had forgotten that Mady had another daughter besides the two that had been witch-stolen. *I have a sister,* Isabelle told herself.

Ravyn had called Honey fat, which she was not, though there was more meat on her bones than on anyone else in the cottage. *More soft than fat,* Isabelle thought, and supposed it was a look that the boys of the village would appreciate. She knew instinctively that when she herself developed a woman's figure, it would most likely be all bony and sharp angles.

Orsen muttered, as though for Ravyn, but loud enough for everyone to hear, "*Honey* definitely for the color of her hair, not for sweetness."

"Oh, Orsen," Honey said, "you're just so precious." She moved in from the doorway then, as though to approach her mother and her maybe-sister Isabelle. But as she passed Orsen, she shot her elbow out, catching him sharply on the side of the head.

Now, THAT, Isabelle thought, *would have hurt.*

"Oops, sorry," Honey said as Orsen staggered.

Ravyn threw herself onto the floor by Hercules Turnip's side, a buffer between the mother who was nursing her pups and all those extra feet in the room.

Honey ignored Orsen, Ravyn, and the dogs, as she studied Isabelle.

Is there any sisterly resemblance? Isabelle wondered. She had looked at her own reflection while fetching water from the barrel that morning, but she had felt vain—and foolish—doing it and had not lingered lest anyone catch her at it. Besides, even a princess with a great deal of time on her hands for gazing into mirrors would know other people's faces better than her own. Still, Isabelle didn't think the girl standing before her now looked at all like the image that had been reflected in the water.

Honey must not have recognized anything in Isabelle's features, either. "I don't think she's Isabelle, no matter what she says. She doesn't look a bit like Isabelle did. She's just trying to get into our family."

Isabelle was taken by surprise. *What an odd thing to say.*

"First of all," Isabelle said, "I never claimed to be Isabelle." She couldn't think of a "second of all" except that already—so soon after their meeting—she didn't like the idea of having Honey as a sister.

"Of course she looks like Isabelle," Mady insisted. "Look at the color of her eyes. Eyes don't change like hair does."

"Just about everyone in the village has brown eyes," Honey said. "Ravyn has brown eyes. Orsen has brown eyes. Even the stupid dog has brown eyes."

Hercules Turnip barked.

"Honey, that's enough," Mady told her eldest daughter. "She looks like her great-aunt Isabelle who she was named after."

Isabelle could see Avis reflecting on this, but couldn't tell what conclusion she came to.

If I had my choice of families, she thought, *I'd prefer Avis and Browley and Ravyn.*

But people don't get to choose their families.

Just then Browley came in, with another man.

"Father," Honey said, "talk some sense into Mother. Tell her this . . . this girl . . . does not look anything like Isabelle." Contemptuously, she added, "*Ravyn* looks more like Isabelle than this one does."

The man, another farmer, judging by the dirt ground into both his clothes and his skin, looked at Mady. He must have come running, for he was a bit out of breath, and he wiped the sweat off his brow with his sleeve, leaving a muddy streak.

Mady put her hand under Isabelle's chin and said, "Look, Frayne. She looks the image of what your father's sister must have been at this age."

Frayne took his direction from his wife, not his daughter.

He looked at Isabelle and said, "Welcome back, Isabelle. We had feared the worst. I'm sure you have a tale to tell. Did you see your baby sister while the old witch held you captive?"

"No," Isabelle said. "I don't remember seeing anyone."

"Honestly!" Honey said, tossing her hair and stomping out of the cottage.

The man, Frayne, had tears in his eyes as he came up to Isabelle and Mady, and he gathered them into his arms. "Well, getting one of you back is more than we ever hoped for. We're here to take you home."

Home.

Honey stuck her head back in the doorway and said, "Oh, just wait another six or seven years, and maybe another girl will show up claiming to be the baby."

"I never claimed . . ." Isabelle started, but Frayne gave Mady and Isabelle another squeeze, and she stopped talking because her words would have been muffled by his arms in any case.

Over his shoulder she saw Avis glance at Browley. Browley shrugged. Orsen was still rubbing the side of his head where Honey had jabbed him, and Ravyn was sitting on the floor patting Hercules Turnip's head.

Isabelle, Isabelle thought. *I'm Isabelle.*

Things were moving too fast.

Still, she would be Isabelle, until—unless—she found out differently.

CHAPTER 6

Somehow, even though Mady and Frayne had talked about taking her home, Isabelle was surprised at how quickly they wanted to leave.

Home.

She had known from the beginning that staying at the cottage of Avis, Browley, and Ravyn had been temporary—*they* had not misplaced a girl her age. They had taken her in only because they were kind people.

"Seeing your old house will do wonders for you," Browley assured her. "Being back in those familiar surroundings will rouse your memory in no time."

Browley had been wrong before.

Avis gave her a fierce hug and whispered into her ear, "And you can come back for a visit whenever you want. *Whenever*. Or to stay longer, should you decide they're mistaken."

Mistaken?

Surely that would be a bad thing. If Mady and Frayne were

mistaken, that would mean starting all over again: no family, no name.

Isabelle felt both relieved at Avis's words and guilty for feeling relieved. But, for a girl with no memory, it was hard to say good-bye to all that was familiar.

Ravyn cried, the only one of Isabelle's new friends who made no attempt to look happy, since even Orsen worked at putting on a smile, though it wasn't much of one. Ravyn threw her arms around Isabelle and buried her face in Isabelle's chest until Avis finally pried Ravyn's fingers loose and said, "Hush now, child. It's not like you'll never see her again. They're only on the other side of the village, not that far a walk."

"No more tears," Browley said, sweeping his granddaughter up into his arms, "or we'll have to put you out with the chickens."

But this time the playful threat didn't make Ravyn giggle, and she hid her face in the angle of her grandfather's neck and shoulder, and she refused to say good-bye.

"Fine," Mady said. "Now that's over." She flung her arm possessively around Isabelle and moved her toward the door.

My mother, Isabelle reminded herself. *My mother, who lost me to the witch, but then I came back.*

Somehow.

Orsen stepped out of the way. Looking at Isabelle, he inclined his head toward Honey, waiting outside, and mouthed the words, *Watch out*. Just in case his meaning wasn't clear, he pointed to his own elbow, then the side of his head where Honey had jabbed him, then once more indicated Honey, and nodded solemnly.

Isabelle nodded also, to let him know she understood, but she had to fight not to smile, knowing he was trying to be helpful.

Frayne pumped Browley's arm. "Thank you," he said, "thank you for taking care of our Isabelle for us."

Browley's hunting dogs began to bark as soon as everyone came outdoors, and that made Isabelle's leg ache again. Her knee buckled, and Mady grabbed her arm to keep her from falling.

Browley said, "The lass probably won't be able to walk all the way. Here, why don't you take the cart?"

The cart was meant for transporting vegetables. There were two poles for someone to stand between and pull, and two big wheels, which were a bit wobbly from going over the rows in the fields. The whole thing was too big and bulky to be easily turned upside down to dump out all the leaves and clumps of dirt, so instead Browley and Frayne picked out the larger pieces of debris and wiped the bottom clean the best they could. Mady fluttered. Honey sighed.

Then Avis spread out the blanket Isabelle had been using—"So your bones won't knock around quite so much," she said.

Isabelle put her hands on the edge of the cart to climb in,

but Frayne came up behind her, lifted her, and gently set her inside. She started at his unexpected help, and she had to fight the impulse to tell him she was perfectly capable of climbing into a cart by herself.

She said, "Thank you," but couldn't bring herself to say, "Father."

The sides of the cart came up almost to her shoulders, but at least she was able to look out. "All right then?" Frayne asked.

Isabelle nodded, not quite trusting her voice yet.

Honey said, "Hmph!" and tossed her curly honey-colored hair over her shoulder. She turned her back to them and began walking, Isabelle could only presume, in the direction of home. And if Orsen hadn't moved out of her way, Honey would have walked right over him.

Home.

That thought would take some getting used to.

Home, Isabelle repeated to herself. The home that something or someone—probably the old witch—had stolen from her.

Ravyn had run back inside the cottage as soon as her grandfather had set her down on the ground when he went to fetch the cart, and she refused to come back out, even now when her grandmother went to the door and announced that Isabelle was about to leave.

"Good-bye!" Isabelle called to all of them, called loud enough for Ravyn to hear, just in case.

Ravyn *still* wouldn't come out.

Frayne picked up the poles and began pulling the cart. Isabelle grabbed the sides to keep from jostling around in there like a loose onion.

The ride was a bit smoother once they got to the actual road, where Honey was waiting for them. Isabelle turned for one last look.

Ravyn burst out of the house, apparently unable to sulk any longer. "Good-bye, good-bye!" she yelled. "Hercules Turnip will miss you!"

Isabelle wished she could return to give Ravyn a hug, but she knew it wasn't fair to ask Frayne to pull the wagon back to the cottage. And he didn't offer.

In the front yard, Browley hoisted Ravyn onto his shoulders, and she waved madly.

Isabelle waved back.

Honey was suddenly right beside her, leaning in close to hiss, "Her royal highness, bidding farewell to her loyal subjects. What a touching scene. Just like from a sad song."

There hadn't been an opportunity for Ravyn to tell Honey her Isabelle-is-a-princess theory, so this jibe must have been in response to Isabelle's getting to ride rather than walk.

Isabelle didn't know what to say. *Maybe we could set the dogs on you, and then you could ride, too?*

Mady, walking beside Frayne, wasn't close enough to have heard Honey's words. Now she turned around and smiled to see the two girls. "Honey and Isabelle. How precious to have them both back together again. Getting reacquainted, my dears?"

"No, Mother," Honey said in a sweet tone that reminded Isabelle of . . . well, honey. Sticky, cloying honey. "I'm just introducing myself."

While Mady looked as though she were trying to work that out, Honey lowered her voice again to speak only to Isabelle. "I don't know what your plan is, but it won't work."

"I don't have a plan," Isabelle said. "Your parents are the ones who say I'm Isabelle. I never did. I can't remember who I am; so maybe I am, and maybe I'm not."

"*Not*," Honey spat out.

"What makes you so sure?"

Honey narrowed her eyes. "Oh, you think you're so clever. Get me to tell you things only I know, so that you can come up with more stories and excuses and not be caught out." She mimicked Isabelle in a voice that Isabelle *knew* she didn't sound like: "Oh, I can't remember a thing. Woe is me. Please take care of me, and if I don't know things I *should* know—why that's because of that convenient loss-of-memory thing. Not because I'm, for example, a lying scoundrel and impostor."

If you know things, Isabelle thought, *why don't you just say them?* But she didn't want to cause a fight, especially not moments after being reunited—maybe—with her family. Instead, she said, "Well, if you think one thing, and they"—she nodded to include Mady and Frayne, whom she didn't know whether to call *your* or *my* parents—"think something else, why don't we seek out someone else to settle it, someone who has known your family for a long time and would recognize if I'm your sister or not."

She hadn't thought Mady was close enough to hear, but Mady had slowed down and now she said, "That's an excellent idea! We'll stop at Isabelle's house."

Honey must have seen the confusion on Isabelle's face. "*Great-aunt* Isabelle. That you're named after. Rich Great-aunt Isabelle—whose money *I* know you're after."

"Ah," Isabelle said.

It didn't sound familiar, but it explained a lot.

CHAPTER 7

Great-aunt Isabelle had a house in the village itself—not on the outskirts, like Avis and Browley at one end, and Mady and Frayne at the far end. The village was named Thornstowe, a name Isabelle thought she knew, once she heard it. The place looked familiar, but Isabelle couldn't be sure if that was because it was *her* village or because most villages look much the same.

As Frayne pulled the cart with Isabelle in it, villagers came up to them. Some, assuming the best, asked Mady and Frayne and Honey if they had heard anything, if anyone had news of the witch or the stolen baby. Others, fearing the worst, offered condolences.

Mady thanked one and all, and said, "We haven't given up hope. But there's hardly a woman among us who hasn't lost a child to sickness or mischance—which is why the midwives always say not to grow too attached until the child has grown old enough to walk and talk, for then it is more likely to survive."

This was such common-sense advice, that Isabelle, too, knew she'd heard it—though, of course, she couldn't remember where.

Then Mady would say, "Still, what the midwives tell us and what our hearts tell us are two different things. All we can do is pray our little babe wasn't in the cottage when it burned, and that we will find her yet. For here is Isabelle back, and we had thought *she* was gone forever. Now she is our comfort in this terrible time."

A few of the villagers smiled at Isabelle, saying, "Welcome back, child." But many looked at Mady with an expression that made Isabelle think they suspected Mady might not be someone whose judgment should be trusted. Isabelle noted these looks and stored them in her heart.

"There," Mady said, as Frayne drew the vegetable cart to a stop in front of the grandest house on the street. It was made of stone, not wood like the other town houses, or wattle and daub like the farm cottages. Mady told Isabelle, "I imagine *this* is a place you know, after all the happy hours you've spent here."

Isabelle saw that Honey was watching with hungry expectation—ready, Isabelle knew, for her to make a mistake.

She started to shake her head, but Mady wouldn't allow her to say she didn't recognize the place. "Well, of course, you will be more accustomed to the inside than the outside. You must recall the tapestry your great-grandmother Helen embroidered, with the scene of the Nativity? Remember how—of all things—it was the little yellow bird in the rafters of the stable that was always your favorite? Most people wouldn't even have noticed that bird, but you always called that tapestry 'the bird tapestry.' And the green bowl that Aunt Isabelle's husband, Warford, gave her so long ago as a betrothal gift? She always keeps it on the table, the table that has that mark where Honey knocked over the candle that time when she was eight, and the flame singed the wood. And—"

"Mother!" Honey interrupted. At first Isabelle thought Honey was embarrassed to have her mother sharing this story of childhood clumsiness. Then Honey said, "*See* if she remembers—don't tell her everything."

Mady laughed. "Don't be silly, Honey. This is not a *test*. We're trying to *help* Isabelle to remember."

Isabelle thought, *I need more than a little help*, since the things Mady was saying did not jostle any memory in her head.

By that time, someone had opened the door to Frayne's knock.

Not the great-aunt. Isabelle could tell without knowing what the great-aunt looked like. This was a girl hardly older than Isabelle, and—judging by the way she curtsied, and by the spills and splatters of food on her apron—she must be the scullery maid.

"Good day, Master Frayne, Mistress Mady." To Honey, she gave a slight bob, not a full curtsy. "Mistress Honey." Finally her gaze lit on Isabelle. Twelve-year-old girls in vegetable carts were obviously a social situation beyond anything the maid had been trained to respond to. She stood on the stoop, swaying slightly, as though evaluating whether to curtsy, dip, or run away.

Ever since they'd entered Thornstowe, Mady had been stopping people to introduce them to Isabelle. Yet now here was someone who truly appeared curious, and Mady was ignoring her. That was something else for Isabelle to take note of, and not know what to do with.

Then suddenly Frayne was by Isabelle's side again, reaching into the cart, lifting her up.

He really should stop doing that, she thought. She knew he was only trying to be helpful, but he made her feel feeble and useless, which was not a feeling she cared for.

Frayne carried her to the door, past the startled maid, and into the house. There were rugs on the floor and tapestries on each of the walls, so that there would be no drafts when the cold winds blew on winter days. And there was furniture of finely crafted wood, furniture that didn't look as if it had been made by people whose primary occupation was farming.

"Aunt Isabelle!" Frayne called out, which almost made Isabelle jump straight out of his arms, both from the loudness and because of the sound of her name, her new name.

She wished he'd set her on her feet, but apparently he wanted to present her to his aunt as if Isabelle were a box of treats or a bouquet of flowers, despite the fact that he was holding her like an oversized bag of cabbages.

In another moment the old woman entered, walking with a thick length of stick to steady herself. "Frayne," she said, "I can't hear half the people in this village, but still *you* hurt my ears."

Isabelle immediately noted that the great-aunt didn't lean heavily on her cane and—in fact—seemed to use it more to bang on the floor for emphasis, or to point.

"Aunt Isabelle!" Mady said. She, also, spoke overly loudly and distinctly. "Look who is here!" And, rather than giving the old woman a chance to guess, Mady continued, "It's Isabelle, your godchild, your namesake, safely returned after all this time, with no more serious an injury than a dog bite."

Whatever the great-aunt had been doing before their arrival, she seemed cranky about the interruption. "Woman," she said to Mady, "it's hard to keep track of your children, with all their comings and goings."

This struck Isabelle as uncommonly harsh, and indeed Mady burst into loud weeping.

Frayne set Isabelle on her feet so fast she had to put her hand out to grasp the table to keep from swaying. "There, there, my sweet," Frayne said, rushing to hold Mady. "She didn't mean that the way it sounded."

Isabelle wondered how else the great-aunt could have meant her statement besides how it sounded. But at the same time, she was distracted because when she'd grabbed hold of the table, her hand had accidentally shoved against something. She looked, to make sure she wasn't knocking things to the floor within moments of getting here.

She found that what she was touching was a green bowl, but fortunately she had pushed it farther onto the table rather than closer to the edge. For an instant she wondered why the bowl hadn't been centered, but then she saw that it had been covering a darkened indentation on the table. She ran her fingers across the wood and realized it was the scorch mark Mady had talked about. And this must be the bowl, the betrothal gift. Isabelle wondered: *had* she ever seen either before, or did she know these things from Mady's description? She looked up—and caught the great-aunt watching her.

Meanwhile, Honey folded her arms across her chest and glared at the old woman, and when the great-aunt saw this, she said to her grandniece, "Hardhearted thing."

Honey tossed her hair and stomped out of the room, practically knocking over the scullery maid, who had lingered in the doorway too long.

They heard the front door slam as Honey left the house.

The great-aunt came up to Isabelle and peered into her face. Nearsighted or scrutinizing, Isabelle couldn't be sure. Age had bent the old woman's back, but Isabelle suspected it hadn't made her mind slow. "So," the great-aunt said, "you're Isabelle."

"I don't know," Isabelle admitted.

The woman's bristly gray eyebrows shot up in surprise.

Mady stopped crying long enough to say, "She is. You can recognize her eyes. And she has your smile."

"Nonsense!" the great-aunt snapped. "Or rather, she might have my smile, but I no longer do. My smile fell out of my mouth years ago." She bared her gums at Isabelle, and indeed she had only about seven teeth.

Isabelle showed her own teeth, which were all there.

Mady, eager to make peace, said, "All right, then. She smiles the way you used to when you still had teeth. Show her, Isabelle."

Apparently this meant Isabelle's toothy grin wasn't right. She tried to smile more naturally, but couldn't do it with everyone watching, including the great-aunt, hardly a handspan away from her face. Isabelle licked her lips and said, "I can't."

The great-aunt snorted, but then she added, "I don't blame you. The world doesn't give much to smile about. So, where have you been all this while? Just waiting for my nephew and his wife to have another baby to name Isabelle?"

The new baby was named Isabelle, too? How many Isabelles were there in this family?

Still sniveling in Frayne's arms, Mady protested, "We wouldn't have named the new baby Isabelle!"

Once again the great-aunt snorted. She told Isabelle, "Maybe, maybe not. But I can't believe they would put up with a dreadful old biddy like me if I didn't have so many nice things."

Despite herself, Isabelle found the great-aunt more agreeable for so freely admitting to being disagreeable.

Mady said, "Frayne and I worry about you, Aunt Isabelle, all alone, with us being your only living family."

The great-aunt leaned in close to Isabelle and said—as if confiding a secret, though she never lowered her voice—"Of course, I suspect she is most worried about my house. Her heart breaks with the thought that my furnishings will be orphaned upon my death. After my husband and son died—both on the same evil day—that's when Mady's concern for me blossomed. If she could have changed Honey's name to Isabelle—in my honor—I have no doubt she would have. But Honey was already four by then. Still, within another two years, she was fortunate enough to have another child—which may or may not be you—and she named that one after me. Of course, Mady was so determined to honor me, I do believe she would have given my name to whatever child came. So be glad you were born a girl."

The great-aunt looked Isabelle up and down appraisingly.

DOES she recognize me? Isabelle wondered. Already she felt more inclined to trust Great-aunt Isabelle's judgment than Mady and Frayne's.

If the old woman came to a conclusion, she didn't share it. She simply said, "Little Isabelle was my delight, for all that I knew why Mady had made her my namesake. But the child wandered off, or was stolen away by the witch in the forest, if rumor be believed. Yet lo and behold, hardly a day after a second child is taken, here you are, miraculously returned to us."

Since the great-aunt was speaking so forthrightly, Isabelle did also. "Well," she said, "we don't know that for sure. I mean, yes, obviously I'm here, but we don't know for sure that I'm Isabelle."

The great-aunt's eyebrows practically joined her hairline.

"Yes we do," Mady called over, still within the embrace of Frayne's arms. Frayne seemed reluctant to let her go, perhaps judging it best to keep his wife out of the range of Great-aunt Isabelle's cane. Mady repeated, "Yes, we do know she's Isabelle."

"No we don't," Isabelle insisted.

"Well, however this works out," the great-aunt told her, "I like you the better for saying that. How is it that you don't know whether you're my grandniece?"

"I have no memory earlier than yesterday morning," Isabelle said, "right before Browley's dogs set upon me in the woods. Avis and Browley's granddaughter, Ravyn, thinks the old witch who lived in the woods may have put a spell on me, and I have no better explanation."

Old as dirt,
dirty as dirt.
Ugly as sin,
mean as sin.
Don't let the old witch catch you!

The singsong words chased one another around inside Isabelle's head. *Had* the old witch caught her?

Mady said, "We always suspected she'd stolen Isabelle, so it can't be just chance that this girl, bearing such an uncanny resemblance to our little girl, should show up, with no memory, on the very day the old witch was trapped in her cottage and burned."

"But if the old witch was trapped," the great-aunt asked Isabelle, "how did *you* chance to escape?"

Isabelle had no answer, but Mady did. "The old witch must have bound her by a spell—that was how she kept her all these years. That way, she could set tasks for Isabelle outdoors without fear of her running away: gathering firewood, collecting mushrooms, searching for herbs. So Isabelle wasn't there when the villagers came and set fire to the cottage where the old witch was hiding. But when the witch died, the spell itself was destroyed."

Mady hadn't mentioned the lost infant. Yet how could the old witch have been burned and the baby not? Wasn't it both or neither?

Mady's thoughts seemed to finally catch up with her words. The color drained from her face, and she gasped, her hand flying to cover her mouth.

"Or not," Frayne said, and it seemed that it was only his hold that kept his wife on her feet after her knees had obviously gone unsteady. "The old witch doesn't need to be dead.

She may have been gone already, as they said she was, before they got to her house. She may have taken our baby and run so far that her spell over Isabelle could no longer stretch and reach to cover Isabelle."

So fast? Isabelle wondered. *Could an old witch and an infant travel so quickly that pursuers couldn't catch up with them? Maybe. Maybe the witch had used magical means to escape, wishing herself and the stolen child away to a far-off land where no one would know them or recognize what the witch was—or what she had done.*

But Isabelle wondered, *If the witch had such a power, why hadn't she used it years before—to carry Isabelle herself off, where there would be no chance of discovery?*

Still, it was a better explanation than anything Isabelle had come up with.

"Maybe," Isabelle said.

"Maybe," the great-aunt agreed.

"Yes," Mady proclaimed, beginning to regain her color. She smiled gratefully at Frayne.

Of course she doesn't want to give up hope about the baby, Isabelle thought. *But neither does she want to give up hope about the great-aunt's inheritance.*

"Look around," Mady instructed Isabelle. "See if the surroundings don't prick at your memory. Notice the tapestry." She waved her hand at the wall to Isabelle's left.

It was the needlework of the Nativity that Mady had mentioned earlier, so Isabelle's gaze went immediately to the upper right-hand corner, where the rafters of the stable had been stitched, and there was the little yellow bird Mady had told her about, so friendly and yellow and fuzzy that Isabelle had to smile.

"See!" Mady said. "She knew to look for the bird. Did you see, Frayne?"

"Yes, my dear," Frayne said.

The great-aunt gave her nearly toothless smile and whispered to Isabelle, "I embroidered that picture while awaiting the birth of my son."

"But . . ." Isabelle said, "but I thought Great-grandmother Helen made it."

"There!" Mady cried. "I told you your memories would come back!"

"But you told me about the tapestry," Isabelle protested, for it wasn't fair to have Great-aunt Isabelle think otherwise.

Mady said, "Of course I did. I told you stories about the family from the time you were tiny. It's important for a child to know about her background. You always asked, 'And then what happened, Mama?' as though I was telling you tales of kings and queens and noble deeds. Remember how I told you about your great-uncle Warford and how he so bravely died saving—"

Isabelle stamped her foot—her right one that didn't hurt. She could see how the great-aunt found her cane so handy for thumping on the ground to gain access to a conversation. "But you told the story about the tapestry me just outside Auntie's door."

"Did I?" Mady asked, but at the same moment Great-aunt Isabelle gasped.

The old woman demanded, "Did she tell you to call me that?"

Isabelle shrank away from the intensity on the great-aunt's face. Gone was the smirk the old lady had been wearing all through the visit, the I'm-relishing-making-fun-of-you expression that clearly indicated she didn't trust anyone or take anything too seriously. Isabelle said, "I'm sorry if I said something improper or upsetting."

"What's wrong?" Mady asked. "Whatever it was, I'm sure the child didn't mean it."

Great-aunt Isabelle waved the cane in Mady's direction to indicate silence. To Isabelle, she said, "My grandniece always called me Auntie, even though Mady instructed her to be more formal, and to call me. . ." In a pompous, rolling voice, she intoned, "Great-aunt Isabelle." She sniffed. "As though it was impeccable manners that would win me over and make me more likely to leave my fortune to her. But when we were alone . . ." She took a deep breath. "Isabelle was always so earnest and truthful. Just the way you've been." She gripped Isabelle's arm, the bony fingers tight enough to hurt. "It *is* you, isn't it? Somehow. It's you: you were stolen away, but *somehow* you've been returned. And you remember me. Oh, Isabelle." Incredibly, she held her arms open.

For a moment, Isabelle considered whether this acceptance might be a trap, whether in another moment the old lady would point at her and say, *See! She can't truly be Isabelle because . . .*

Because what? Because the child Isabelle never hugged people? Because she was always contrary? Because in truth she had never called the great-aunt Auntie?

Nothing really fit.

Except that Great-aunt Isabelle's doubts had been laid to rest, and now she accepted Isabelle as her grandniece.

Isabelle searched her mind, but didn't find either Great-aunt Isabelle or Auntie there. Surely Auntie wasn't so uncommon a title that it should be proof.

Still, she liked that a cranky, suspicious old woman who'd had every reason to distrust her when Mady had thrown them together had, instead, loved her.

This was so much more probable than being a princess, so much less scary than being an animal.

She wanted to believe. She wanted to belong. She wanted to resume a normal life, *her* normal life.

But she didn't want to lie—to others or to herself.

Yet, while Isabelle hesitated, thinking about all this, Auntie came over to her and hugged her and whispered hoarsely in her ear, "Oh, welcome back, child!"

CHAPTER 8

Just as things were getting interesting, just as Isabelle was beginning to feel that maybe—maybe—she had found, if not her memories, at least her family, Mady said it was time for them to go home—"Lest Isabelle grow weary."

This took Isabelle by surprise, since at no point during the trip or the visit had Mady asked how she was feeling, just as she had never asked whether Isabelle was up to leaving Avis and Browley's home in the first place. All of which made Isabelle suspect that the sudden urgency to leave had less to do with herself and more to do with Mady not wanting Auntie to start asking difficult questions.

But Isabelle couldn't find a way to put into words all the conflicting things she felt. Not to mention those she suspected. Or hoped. Or feared.

It would be so nice to have found her home, to anticipate having her memories gradually return as she found herself in her accustomed setting, surrounded by family.

Of course, *if* Great-aunt Isabelle was Auntie, then along with that, Mady was Mother, and Frayne was Father.

And that would also mean Honey was elder sister.

Auntie said, "Perhaps the child has traveled as much as she should for the day and could spend the night here so she doesn't tire herself returning to your house?"

But Mady was firm. "After being away for so long, I'm sure it would be best for her to be among the more familiar surroundings of her own home. That's without doubt the best way to refresh her memory."

Auntie patted Isabelle's hand, then let it go.

Isabelle found herself disconcerted to have people making decisions about her.

As Frayne approached, looking ready to hoist her up yet again, Isabelle took control of the only thing she could and said, "I think I can make it to the door on my own."

He hovered, just in case her leg gave out, even though she had walked around Avis and Browley's cottage the better part of the day without falling and had even managed to fix the noonday meal for the family. Still, his concern was sweet—if a bit overpowering. And she did need his assistance, after all, getting back into the cart.

On the street, there was no sign of Honey, and Isabelle wondered if she had gone home—and also wondered if Honey's *home* was still with her parents. At almost eighteen, she was old enough to be wed, but her manner, Isabelle felt, was of an older child, not of a married woman.

As Frayne pulled the cart, Mady walked close enough to start telling Isabelle all about the family. She started with Great-uncle Warford, who was not one of Isabelle's primary concerns since he had died so long ago that—even if she *were* his grandniece—she had never met him. But Mady said, "Let me refresh your memory," which Isabelle translated into: *Let me tell you enough that your ignorance of family matters won't be an embarrassment.*

Mady said: "Your great-uncle Warford was a game warden for Lord Cranston. Aunt Isabelle was a maid—hard to believe with her uppity ways, I know—and their only son, Kemp, was also in service to the family. Warford and Kemp died—very bravely—while rescuing the lord's young wife. It happened while the household was moving from their winter estate to their summer holdings. Spring rains had washed out the road, just where it follows the river, but high above. The lady's wagon started to go over the edge and was about to fall hundreds of feet into the raging water below. The lady was paralyzed by fear and could not climb through the door Warford held open for her. Kemp crawled into the wagon to help. As Warford pulled from one direction, Kemp pushed from the other, until they got the lady free. But no sooner had this been done than the wagon tipped over the slippery edge and crashed down the ravine, taking Kemp with it. Warford heard his son's death cry, but there was nothing he could do except tighten his grip on the lady. He handed her off to another servant, higher up on the road—then the very next moment he himself lost his footing and fell to his death."

Auntie *had* said it was an evil day.

Isabelle, who—until such a short time ago—had had no family, wondered how one survived such a loss. She was left saddened and empty, though she had never met Warford or Kemp. That's what family did: it provided ties—for good or ill.

Mady continued, "The lady was grateful for her own life and regretted their deaths. She showered your great-aunt with costly gifts—and rightly so. Of course, all the riches in the world couldn't ever take the place of Kemp and Warford, but the lord and lady's benevolence made Aunt Isabelle's life more comfortable. Not that Aunt Isabelle was the only one who grieved. *We*, too, mourned their passing. And I don't know what the nuns of the abbey of Saint Verbena have ever done—besides offer up a few prayers for Warford and Kemp's souls—that Aunt Isabelle should leave her money to them, as she has declared it her intention to do."

Isabelle stopped listening as Mady chattered on.

For all Isabelle knew, Mady *may* have been her mother; and she may well have been a kind and loving mother who had been inconsolable for the loss of two of her children. But Auntie's wealth was at least one reason why Mady might be yearning for Isabelle to be that long-lost child.

Meanwhile Auntie was so desperate to have her grandniece

back that she was willing to overlook any inconsistencies.

As for Frayne, he reminded Isabelle of the kind of puppy that feels its purpose in life is to make its master happy. Frayne wanted Mady to be happy, and so he was willing to accept Isabelle as his daughter without question.

Honey, Isabelle reflected, *is perhaps the most honest of them all in being skeptical.*

Which didn't, of course, make Honey right.

But Isabelle decided she shouldn't dismiss Honey's opinion just because Honey was unpleasant and spiteful.

Honey is convinced I'm out to trick them so I can get at Auntie's wealth. But the one thing I know for sure is that I have not set out to trick anyone.

Surely that gave weight to Mady and Frayne and Auntie's belief that Isabelle's turning up when and where she had could not be a coincidence.

Isabelle interrupted Mady in the midst of another of her family stories. "What happened . . ." Should she ask "to me" or "to Isabelle?" She finished, ". . . six years ago?"

Mady's eyes welled with tears.

This had to have been impossibly hard for her, Isabelle thought, *losing two children. Then, after all this time, seeing someone who may or may not be one of them. Not knowing whether to keep on hoping for the other one, who—after all—has been gone only a day and a half now. The sorrow must be almost unbearable.*

Even if she IS grasping at Great-aunt Isabelle's possessions.

Mady was too complicated. Isabelle guessed she'd never fully understand her.

Isabelle was just wondering how much to press, when Mady told her everything.

"It was a lovely spring afternoon," Mady began, as she gripped the side of the cart, "and I was gathering berries in the woods. You were with me. You always loved the woods—the sounds, the smells, always hoping for a glimpse of a deer or a fox or even a toad or a butterfly. We were walking, talking, still eating almost as many berries as we were gathering. And then, suddenly, something came over me. My eyelids and my feet grew heavy. I could barely keep my eyes open; I couldn't take another step. At the time, I didn't suspect anything was wrong. I thought I was just tired. *Now* I realize the old witch had put a spell on me. 'Let's rest our heads,' I said, 'just for a moment or two.' And I spread my cloak on the ground. I remember both of us lying down, you snuggled in my arms."

Isabelle let the pictures form in her mind: the six-year-old tot feeling happy and secure with her mother. The basket, never getting more than half-full. The berry-stained fingers. The juice—sometimes sweet and sometimes deliciously tart—on her tongue. The fragrance of the forest. The strong arms encircling her protectively.

Mady's voice quavered. "And then I was waking up, and the shadows were long, for it was getting to be evening, and you were gone. I called and called, but you never answered. Honey, bless her heart—only as old then as you are now—had come looking for us because we'd been away for so long, and I sent her home to fetch your father, but still there was no sign of you. Villagers joined in the search. Browley came with his dogs, because he's always had the best hunting dogs, but even they couldn't find you. They led us to a hole where the ground had given way—but you weren't there. The men lowered themselves with ropes, but they couldn't find anything. Some animal the dogs were interested in must have lived in that hole, because they were too distracted to be enticed away to take up your scent again."

Isabelle said, "They found me yesterday." She was thinking about how they had lunged and snapped, frightening her up into a tree, and—whatever else had happened to her—she was glad they hadn't found her when she was only six years old.

But Mady didn't have that connection with the dogs, and she smiled through her tears and agreed, "Yes, they found you yesterday."

"Tell me about the witch," Isabelle said.

"We went to her that night, since her cottage is . . . was . . . not so very far away in the woods. 'Have you seen our little lost girl?' we asked. She'd only opened the door a crack, and at the time we thought it was because she was timid, her with the reputation of being a witch, finding villagers on her doorstep, carrying torches and leading dogs. And she said: 'If I had a child, I would take better care than to lose it in the woods where all manner of creatures might carry it off.' Can you imagine? Saying that to a distressed family? We thought she was cruel. We didn't realize how cruel. We didn't realize *she* was the creature who had carried you off. Do you remember? Do you remember her taking you away?"

Isabelle tried. She pictured waking up in the woods, still in her mother's arms, the witch leaning over her. Then she pictured waking up in the witch's cottage, the witch having brought her there while she was still asleep. But neither image led Isabelle to any real memories.

And why would the witch want her? Again Isabelle looked at her hands, which did not bear the marks of hard work or of beatings.

She asked, "Was it the same with the second child, the one who was taken yesterday?"

"No," Mady said.

While Isabelle waited for Mady to explain, she could hear Frayne's footfalls on the dirt road. He was not listening to their conversation, but was humming to himself, a cheery melody that she recognized as a hymn, a song whose somber words she knew to be at odds with the light tune.

"Here we are," Frayne announced, nodding toward the next house in the row.

"Do you recognize it?" Mady asked expectantly.

The house was low and squat like most of the houses except Auntie's, with fresh thatch on the roof and the smell of lamb stew simmering over the cook fire. Despite her irritation with her parents for taking in Isabelle, Honey must have pulled the pot over the fire.

"No," Isabelle said, then amended that to, "I don't know," since, if nothing else, the place looked similar to others they had passed on the way.

"The inside, then," Mady said. "That will speak *home* to you."

"Tell me about the baby," Isabelle asked in a rush, for she could see Honey through the window opening, and she suspected that Honey would continue to complain that Mady was telling her too much.

Mady took a deep shuddering breath and crossed her arms over her breasts. Talking about the baby, Isabelle suddenly realized, must be causing her breasts to ache with the milk her body was still producing for an infant who was no longer there to drink it. Mady said, "I had left the baby at home with Honey while I was visiting with my friend Edyth. You remember Edyth? She has a peach tree in her yard, so she's always making treats with peaches. You loved her tarts. And you used to play with her daughter, Willa."

"Go on," Isabelle urged her.

"When I came back, the door was open. Honey was on the floor of the kitchen, suffering from convulsions, her eyes rolled up in her head, her limbs all shaking. I knelt beside her, to keep her from banging her head on the floor, and when the fit had passed, her first words were, 'The baby.'"

Isabelle was listening to all this in horror when Frayne stopped pulling the cart and came and stood beside Mady. He didn't say anything, but only watched his wife with eyes large and sad. For the first time, she realized that the reason he and Mady had not talked about this before was not because it wasn't important to them, but because they were so distraught. Suddenly, the great-aunt's jibes were no longer amusing, but mean-spirited.

Mady said, "This time, the witch came right to our house and cast a spell on Honey. I don't know why she has chosen to plague our family. But even while Honey was twitching, helpless, like someone possessed, she had been able to see the witch pick the babe up and steal away with her."

"How awful!" Isabelle said. No wonder Honey was so surly after such an experience.

"The villagers set fire to the old witch's house. They say they broke down the door and saw that she wasn't there, and that they lit the fire to keep her from coming back. Too late did the fools realize that she may have been hiding in there. What did they expect, that she would come to the door to greet them with the babe in her arms? Stupid, stupid fools . . ." Mady's voice disappeared over a tattered edge.

Frayne said, "Mayhap she preferred to die in the flames, taking our daughter with her, rather than let us have her back.

Or mayhap she truly escaped—and we don't know which to pray for, since we don't know what she wanted our little girl for. Our hearts were like to break. But you have healed us, Isabelle. Welcome back."

CHAPTER 9

So this was what it was like to be part of a family.

It was quite a burden to be Isabelle, with her parents' happiness depending on her. She worried about this as they sat in their house, everyone waiting for her to remember.

Well, Frayne and Mady seemed eager for her to remember.

As for Honey. . .

One could never be sure what Honey was thinking.

Theirs was a much simpler house than Auntie's. As with the cottage that Avis and Browley and Ravyn shared, there was only one room, though the parents' bed was curtained off with a length of brown cloth for privacy. The furniture was sparse and rough-hewn, and Isabelle tried to find familiarity in how it was arranged. But she must have been thinking back to Avis and Browley's house, for when she said, "Yes, I remember the bed by the fireplace," Honey snorted and told her, "The bed *I* shared with *my* sister Isabelle used to be on the far wall. It was moved closer to the fireplace *after* she was taken."

Quickly—almost as though to keep Isabelle from making another such mistake—Mady added that the bed's blue woad-dyed blanket had been woven just this past winter since the russet-colored one Isabelle *would* have remembered had become so ragged from use.

"Here's part of it," Mady said, pointing to a piece of wool that was braided into a rug next to Mady and Frayne's bed. "Oh, and in this cap I made for Frayne, too."

Isabelle tried—but it was hard to recognize a blanket from a twisted segment of rug or from a cap.

Of course, the clothes she had worn as a six-year-old had all been taken apart, too, the wool or flax reused to make or mend other items.

Next, Mady showed her a beautiful mirror—made with a real piece of glass, not burnished metal—and an elaborately wrought tortoise-shell comb to match. These were the fanciest things in the house, so most likely the items had been a gift from Auntie, who was the only one in the family who could afford such fine things. The comb that Isabelle saw on Honey's night chest was wooden and plain.

Sitting on the edge of her bed, Mady said, "We used to sit here, while I combed your hair in the morning and at night."

Something tickled the back of Isabelle's memory, so she said, "Yes, I seem to remember that . . . as though it happened long, long ago."

Honey wiped the smile from Mady's face by cooing, "Oooo, a little girl getting her hair combed by her mother. Now *there's* something that can't have happened in very many families."

The stew they had for supper was tasty, but stew was a staple in most households, and there was nothing so distinctive about Mady's as to convince Isabelle she'd had it before.

Afterward, Mady told her, "You sit, dear. I'll clean up." Honey snorted, but when Mady sent a glare in her direction, Honey pretended she'd just been grunting with the effort of bending over for the basket with the sewing.

"Do you remember this, Isabelle?" asked Frayne, who for the most part had stayed out of all the attempts to awaken Isabelle's memory. He held out to her a wooden top, plain and a bit dusty.

Isabelle took it into her hands, thinking it was a toy such as many children had. She asked, "You made this?"

Frayne's face broke out into a grin, and he bobbed his head.

Isabelle said it more definitely: "You made this for me."

Honey said, "He made it for *me*. I just let you play with it." A moment later, she realized what she'd said. She bit back any further comment and ducked her head to indicate she was too busy to engage in conversation anymore, as though the skirt she was mending required all her attention.

In the silence, there was a knock on the door that sounded much too loud. Isabelle jumped, startled. *Surely*, she tried to reassure herself, *danger does not come knocking*. Perhaps someone had brought news of the baby—and that news could be good as easily as bad.

Frayne opened the door to a woman and a girl.

"Edyth!" Mady said, putting down the cloth she had been using to wipe off the table. "And Willa! We were just talking about you earlier." She didn't mention how their names had come up in explaining where Mady had been when the witch had bespelled Honey and stolen the baby.

For a woman who had been described as liking to make peach treats, Edyth was gaunt and even a bit sour looking. When she saw Isabelle, though, her smile transformed her face into looking almost beautiful. "Is this her? This must be Isabelle. Isabelle, welcome home!"

She held her arms out, obviously expecting a hug.

For some reason, returning Edyth's hug didn't seem as difficult as returning Mady's had been. This was, after all, only a friendly neighbor, not a potential mother. Isabelle went to Edyth and put her arms around her. But it wasn't an exuberant hug, for Edyth looked frail, as though her bones might crack from too much enthusiasm. And—despite the fact that she was years younger than Auntie—Edyth, too, carried a stick to help her walk, except hers was a thick stick that she leaned on heavily. However far she'd walked, she seemed out of breath.

Rather than invite Edyth to come all the way in and sit, Frayne brought a stool to her just within the doorway.

"Goodness!" Edyth sat down almost as quickly as if collapsing. She took a few deep breaths before saying, "My, how you've grown, Isabelle. Of course, I expect you think the same of Willa."

Willa had been Isabelle's friend, Mady had said, back . . . before. *It would be good to have a friend,* Isabelle thought, *someone her own age, someone with whom to share time and thoughts.*

The girl who had been helping to support Edyth now looked up at Isabelle. She had curly hair and an expression that hinted she knew both how to cause—and how to get out of—trouble.

Isabelle liked Willa's face, but there was absolutely nothing familiar about it.

"Hello, Isabelle," Willa said. "Do you like my new dress? My mother just finished making it this morning. Well, I mean, we both did some of the spinning and weaving and sewing, but she added the fancy stitching here on the bodice. I think the blue makes my eyes look green, which I really like, but she made the sleeves *so* long. I know they need to be long enough to give me room to grow in, but, still, I'm going to be rolling them up for the next two years, and by then I'll have a bosom, and then the dress will be too tight anyway, and it will be her own fault if the hems of the sleeves get all ragged from dragging around, which I've already told her, but she never listens to me."

No wonder poor Edyth looked worn out.

Isabelle opened her mouth to tell Willa that the dress was

pretty and to assure her that the sleeves looked fine, but Willa had only paused for a breath.

"Mother said we should bring my old dress for you. It's blue, too, but a different shade—it's not that it's ugly, it just never suited me as well as this one does—but, anyway, Mother said maybe we should bring that in case you needed a dress, because . . ." Finally Willa had to actually hunt for a thought, but she didn't hesitate long. "Well, we didn't know what you've been through and what to expect, and we thought you might need it. But I pointed out to Mother that you were always taller than me, so if I'd outgrown the dress, it certainly would be too small for you. But now I see that I've caught up to you, and I'm thinking I might even be taller. Which is a pleasant surprise. Well, it is for me, anyway."

She spun Isabelle so she could stand back-to-back with her and placed her arm across both their heads.

Willa showed the angle at which their heights made her arm tip. "See, I told you. So maybe the dress would fit you after all. Would you like it? I know you can't remember it, because you've been gone six years, and I've only had it since winter before last, but—truly—it isn't repulsive, I hope I didn't give you that impression, it just isn't as attractive as this one, and it's a bit worn"—Willa indicated the sleeve edge—"but not badly enough that it needs to be patched. Do you want to go back to the house and see?"

"Oh, I don't know," Isabelle started, thinking she didn't

know how far away Edyth and Willa lived and remembering how—at Auntie's house—Mady had seemed eager for the family to be home. "Maybe—"

"Please go!" Honey said with a scowl to indicate she found the talkative Willa annoying.

Mady looked hesitant to let Isabelle out of her sight, but Frayne said, "What else are long summer evenings for but to visit with friends?"

So Mady gave in, saying, "Mind you don't overdo with your injured leg."

Willa told Edyth, "We'll be back soon so I can help you home, Mama." Then she hooked her arm around Isabelle's and took her outside. "*Is* your leg injured?" Willa asked her. "I'd hoped to take you by Dunn's house, so you could see Chetwyn."

"Who's Dunn?" Isabelle asked. "Who's Chetwyn?"

"My brother Chetwyn, silly. He's helping Dunn and his father fix the wall of their house where it's sagging because it got so damp this spring. You were always sweet on him."

"I was?" *At six years old?* Isabelle thought. "Dunn or Chetwyn?"

"Chetwyn, you little tease. I have my eye on Dunn, so you can't have him." But Willa was laughing. "You really don't remember anything, do you? I thought you were just making that up so as not to get in trouble."

Isabelle asked, "In trouble for what?"

Still laughing, Willa said, "I don't know. For whatever you did that you didn't want to talk about."

"No," Isabelle told her. "I really can't remember anything." Willa had probably been able to guess already, by the slowness with which Isabelle was walking, that the injury wasn't feigned. The dirt road was dusty and uneven, making walking a bit difficult even under the best of circumstances. Isabelle added, "And my leg really is hurt. One of Browley's dogs bit me."

"Ouch!" Willa said. But she didn't waste good talking time on sympathy. "We used to play together: you, me, and Chetwyn. He's a year older than we are, and not bad looking, for a brother. Since you liked him then, you'll probably still like him now. Dunn is his friend, Summer's brother. If you don't remember Chetwyn, you won't remember Summer—she's a bit younger than we are, so we didn't have much to do with her back then. Except, of course, her brother Dunn was always fine to look at. He's a year older than Chetwyn."

Isabelle was feeling tired already. She said, "Maybe, for today, we should just go directly to your house."

"Too late," Willa said. "We're already going the wrong way. It will give you a chance to see Chetwyn, and I'd really like Dunn and Summer to see my new dress." Willa let go of Isabelle's arm to twirl in the street. "Isn't it lovely? See how it moves so nicely? Do you think Dunn will find me pretty in it?"

"Yes," Isabelle agreed. Then quickly, before Willa started talking again, she asked, "Do you remember me?"

Willa stopped twirling to give Isabelle a quizzical look. "Well, of course I remember, silly. *You're* the one who lost her memory, not me."

"I mean," Isabelle said, "have I changed?"

"Yes," Willa said, dragging the word out as though she'd just realized she was talking with a simpleton. "You're six years older than you were. So am I. So is Chetwyn. So is Dunn. So is Sum—"

"Understood," Isabelle interrupted. "But is it still me? Can you recognize me?"

"Well, who else would you be?" Willa said. She began twirling again, obviously bored by this line of questions.

"Oh, I don't know," Isabelle could have said. "A princess? A badger? A broomstick come to life?"

Isabelle saw that Frayne had been right about neighbors using the extra summer sunlight to visit, for among the cluster of houses that was Thornstowe, the people were all about, strolling and chatting. One of a pair of severe-looking older women called over to Willa, "Young mistress, does your mother need to be told of your foolishness?"

"Oh no, mistress," Willa assured her. "I'm sorry I forgot myself, mistress." She stopped twirling, but obviously found herself dizzy and had to cling to Isabelle to keep her balance. Laughing, still reeling, she whispered to Isabelle, "Although *you're* the one who truly forgot herself." Then she said, "Isabelle, make the world stop spinning." She closed her eyes and swayed. "Is the old biddy gone yet?"

Isabelle squeezed her arm. "Hush," she warned in an urgent whisper, for the two women were approaching.

Willa opened her eyes and made a show of attempting to stand straight.

The two women, however, ignored Willa and fixed their attention on Isabelle. "So," said the one who had already reprimanded Willa, "you're Mady's girl?" She pinched Isabelle's arm as though to check how much meat there was on her.

Before Isabelle could answer, the other said, "She's not Mady's girl. She may have been Mady's girl once, but she's not now. She's the witch's girl now."

The other agreed. "Born of Mady," she proclaimed, "raised by a witch. It's hard to tell *what* she is now."

The thoughts were not new to Isabelle. But hearing the words spoken out loud—*that* was distressing.

As though they assumed Isabelle was incapable of understanding, the women continued to talk about her.

"Do you think the witch specifically trained her to accomplish something and let her loose among us now?"

"Is a witch born or made?"

"Doesn't matter. You don't need to be a witch to do evil."

Isabelle was left speechless, but Willa wasn't. "I beg your pardon," she proclaimed loudly. "Shouldn't you be feeling *sorry* for a victim of a witch?"

"Sorry?"

"Sorry?"

The two women blinked.

"Sorry?" the first woman repeated. "For *her*? I don't think so. *We're* the ones I feel sorry for. No good will come of this."

"Indeed," the other said. "No good at all."

The two walked away, shaking their heads. "She's already having a bad effect on Edyth's daughter," Isabelle heard one of them saying. "Dancing in the street! The idea!"

"I'm sorry," Isabelle told Willa. "Now I've gotten you in trouble."

Willa shrugged. "Those two are always looking for somebody to complain about."

Still, likely there will be more of that, Isabelle thought, for the villagers had every right to be apprehensive when even she herself could not tell what lessons she might have learned from the witch. Though she had no scars on her body, who could guess what scars there might be on her soul?

Old as dirt,
dirty as dirt.
Ugly as sin,
mean as sin.
Don't let the old witch catch you!

"I think I have just about enough energy to get back home," Isabelle said.

"But the boys!" Willa protested.

Isabelle was curious to see a boy so fine that a six-year-old girl could be smitten with him, but she just shook her head.

Reluctantly, Willa took hold of her arm, and the two girls turned around and went back to Mady and Frayne's house—without talking to Chetwyn and Dunn, without showing Willa's new dress to anybody besides the two old biddies, without getting Willa's old dress for Isabelle.

CHAPTER 10

Isabelle and Willa did not tell about their encounter with the suspicious old women of Thornstowe. Willa only announced that Isabelle had grown weary before they'd gotten far, and Edyth proclaimed, "*That* is something I can understand. It's best we return home ourselves, child. You can bring Isabelle the dress tomorrow."

Isabelle should have been pleased to hear that she'd have another chance to see her friend, but it appeared as though—whatever else had happened—the two of them were not as close as they had been. It wasn't that Isabelle didn't like Willa; it was just that they seemed to have so little in common.

Willa seems so young, Isabelle thought, although it seemed disloyal to feel that of someone who had just stood firm and defended her. *Or maybe I'm the one who's not acting my age. Maybe I'm supposed to have my head full of nothing but boys and clothes.*

Meanwhile, as Mady saw the visitors to the door, Frayne

patted Isabelle's head sympathetically, and Honey kept her tight-lipped scowl.

Night approached, with its shadows lurking in corners. This was an opportunity for Isabelle to ask the family, "Was I afraid of the dark?" But—whether their Isabelle had been or not—*this* Isabelle was concerned that admitting to such a fear might give Honey power over her.

So she said nothing and, come night, she shared a bed with Honey. She'd expected that Honey might be mean about it, kicking, or taking all the space. She was not; but she tossed and turned and sighed often.

Isabelle was fairly certain she herself was not used to sharing a bed.

It's been six years, she told herself.

She wondered if the witch had made her sleep on the floor, or even outside, with the animals. She should try that to see if it brought on any memories—but some other time. She couldn't very well get out of bed now, or Honey was sure to reproach her. Isabelle tried to picture herself cold and miserable on the hard floor. Had the mattress she'd used at Avis's house been an unaccustomed treat? Isabelle thought not, but—as usual—couldn't be sure.

As long as she was making plans . . . *Tomorrow I'll go to the neighbors and see if they think I'm Isabelle*, she told herself. *They'll have no particular concern about declaring yes or no.*

Well, except of course for the two she and Willa had met

this evening. She would have to find out who they were and make sure to avoid them.

Still, others—too—might be concerned about a child who had been raised by a witch. They might well declare she wasn't Isabelle in the hope of getting her to leave.

So these were two things to worry about: Was she or wasn't she Isabelle? And was she or wasn't she an evil tool of the witch of the forest?

She tried to make her mind stop whirling and skittering from one thought to another, but her mind wouldn't cooperate, and sleep eluded her.

And so she and the girl who might be her sister lay side by side in the dark, both restless but ignoring each other, waiting for the endless night to be over.

Isabelle awoke when the door slammed shut.

As she jerked awake, she realized that it wasn't only the dark she was afraid of—she was also afraid of someone bursting in to get her.

The hour was shortly past daylight, and what Isabelle had heard was only Honey entering the house, carrying a basket of flowers.

"Oh, sorry," Honey said, and—amazingly—she sounded as though she might mean it. "I couldn't sleep, so as soon as it was light I went to gather some welcome-home flowers for you. I didn't stop to think that you might still be asleep. Everybody else has been up forever. Father's in the field, but Mother said we should let you rest since you needed the extra sleep to heal." Honey put the basket down on the table.

Isabelle wasn't quite sure what to make of Honey's new, friendly manner. She didn't dare say anything for fear of bringing back the sarcastic, sulky girl Honey had been yesterday.

The edges of the older girl's sleeves were dark with wet, which must mean the morning dew had been especially heavy. How unexpectedly sweet of Honey to have gone out in that dampness to pick flowers to make the drab house look prettier. So all Isabelle said was, "Those flowers are beautiful. And they smell wonderful."

"Don't they?" Honey agreed. Hesitantly, she added, "I've been thinking about some of the things that were said yesterday, and I'm beginning to think that maybe you are who you claim to be."

Isabelle didn't correct her—that she had never claimed to be anyone. She'd only *hoped* to find a home.

Honey said, "I'm sorry I was so short with you. I was just trying to keep my parents—our parents—from any more hurt."

The fear of getting hurt. That would probably explain Auntie's caustic temper also. As well as the suspicions of the Thornstowe biddies.

Isabelle nodded to show she understood.

Honey turned away from her to go to the cupboard. "If

you're ready to get up now, I can cut some bread and cheese for you. Why don't you put the flowers in water?"

Isabelle got out of bed and slipped her dress on over her head, while Honey not only set out breakfast for her, but also placed an earthenware jug for the flowers on the table and ladled water into it out of the barrel. "Not quite as fine as Great-aunt Isabelle's precious green bowl," she pointed out. "But we can still try to make the place look nice. Mother is milking the goats. Do you still like milk? Shall I get you some?"

With her eyes and mind still blurred from sleep, Isabelle found Honey's stream of chatter and questions somewhat overwhelming. "Milk would be nice," she said. "I can get—"

"I will." Honey brushed past her toward the door. "You get the flowers before they start to wilt. And the next thing after that will be to see about shortening and taking in one of my dresses for you, since I don't think you should count on Willa's dress fitting you, and the skirt of the one you've been wearing is all ragged."

In this new amiable mood, Honey didn't mention that Isabelle's dress needed a good washing even more than it needed patching.

Honey herself smelled nice, Isabelle thought, of meadow and chamomile soap. It would be pleasant to have an agreeable older sister.

Isabelle went to the table and began to lift the flowers out of the basket one by one. Some were meadow flowers; others were flowers Honey must have gathered in the woods behind the house. Waiting for Honey to return, Isabelle brought the blooms up to her nose and inhaled the fresh fragrance. She liked wildflowers—that was another piece of her past that fell into place. Some had no purpose except to be pretty, but others were useful. Calendula, she noticed; it not only smelled sweet but could make an infusion that would help digestion. Tansy was good for strewing on the floor or tucking between sheets to keep lice and vermin away. One lone sprig of shepherd's purse—well, it was late in the season, but that could stop bleeding.

But then Isabelle's hand froze over the basket. There, among the daisies and sweet William and Scotch broom and lady's-mantle, was a cluster of delicate white blooms that she hoped her hand had not touched.

She started toward the water barrel, then told herself to stop thinking only of herself and went to the door instead. "Honey!" she called.

Honey was coming around the corner, carrying a bucket.

"Honey, come in here immediately," Isabelle said. "You need to wash your hands."

"What?" Honey asked.

Isabelle caught hold of her arm, making sure to grab the fabric of her dress and not her skin, and she could see that Honey's sleeve was damp up to the elbow. Isabelle dragged her inside so quickly that some of the milk splashed out of the bucket.

"Careful," Honey told her.

"We need to wash," Isabelle ordered. "There's blister weed in that basket."

Honey said slowly, "No, I picked columbine and angelica and cow parsnip and . . ."

Isabelle let go of her to pour water on her own hands. "Soap," she demanded.

Honey pointed it out to her.

Isabelle rubbed the soap onto her hands and arms, then held it out to Honey.

But still Honey seemed unconvinced of the urgency of the situation. "That's not blister weed. That's cow parsnip."

"That would be smaller," Isabelle said. She tried not to sound scornful, but Honey's ignorance had endangered them all. "And the hairs around the stem would be finer. Besides, it's too late in the season for cow parsnip. You're just lucky you picked the flowers while the sun was still low in the sky."

Sap from blister weed could sit harmlessly on someone's hands or arms all night long, but once sunlight touched where the flowers or the stems had come into contact with the skin, the sap would eat into that unlucky person's flesh.

What was the matter with Mady not to have educated Honey about what was and what wasn't safe to touch?

Isabelle said, "If you don't get that off you, within two days, you'll have blisters as though you'd leaned against the heated cooking pot. And they'll never heal properly. And if you get it anywhere near your eyes—Honey, you haven't rubbed your eyes, have you?"

"No," Honey said. She'd finally started to wash her hands, though she was still moving infuriatingly slowly.

Isabelle wasn't even sure her hand had brushed the deadly blooms, and she was scrubbing until her skin was red. Honey had *picked* the flowers.

Obviously, Honey didn't understand the danger. Wasn't the risk of blister weed common wisdom around here? Isabelle didn't know where she herself had gained the knowledge about how noxious blister weed could be, but Honey needed to be convinced. "Here, rub your skin with this cloth," Isabelle said.

"All right." Honey was beginning to get that old sulky tone back to her voice.

Just then Mady walked in. She started to say, "Good mor—" but then she saw the two girls washing their hands, lather up to their elbows. "What are you doing?" she asked.

"Honey picked blister weed," said Isabelle.

Honey insisted, "*I* think it's cow parsnip."

"Better safe than sorry," Mady told them. "Remember how Hadwin got into a batch of that stuff two years ago? He didn't know until the sun brought out the blisters the next day, and by then it was too late. The blisters got so bad, he looked like he'd rolled into a fire pit. He went blind by the third day, then the infection went into his blood, and he died from it."

"All right, all right," Honey said, scrubbing her hands. "I

don't know how someone who doesn't know her own name knows so much about what is and what isn't blister weed."

Mady took a rag—it was a remnant from the russet-colored blanket—and, being careful not to touch the stems directly, picked up the whole assortment of flowers and tossed them into the cook fire. Then, though her hands had been protected, she joined the girls at the washbowl to clean her hands, too, just to be certain.

Isabelle looked at Honey. Since they'd had a neighbor die of it, Honey knew how toxic the sap of blister weed could be. How could she be so calm? Why wasn't she frantic?

Still watching Honey, Isabelle dried her hands and arms. She'd pushed up the sleeves of her dress, but they'd still gotten soaked from her washing.

Just as Honey's sleeves had been soaked when she'd walked in.

When she'd walked in, smelling of soap.

She'd already washed her hands, Isabelle realized.

But that didn't make any sense. Why would Honey have washed her hands unless she'd known it was blister weed? And if she'd known it was blister weed, why had she picked it and pretended not to know?

But it *did* make sense.

It was just that Isabelle didn't want to believe it.

CHAPTER 11

Why would Honey intentionally try to harm her? At the least, blister weed would cause pain and disfiguring scars. At the worst . . . Though her memory could come up with no other names, Isabelle knew that the death of their neighbor Hadwin wasn't the first death she had heard attributed to the baneful plant.

Honey turned from washing her hands, and their eyes met. Isabelle glanced away, pretending she had not been looking at the elder girl, pretending that her gaze had only chanced to pass over Honey at that particular moment. But Honey wasn't fooled. Isabelle could feel Honey staring at her. Honey *knew* that she knew.

The smoke from the burning flowers hung heavy in the air, stinging Isabelle's eyes and making Mady cough. Isabelle understood how Mady had been eager to get rid of the blister weed, but throwing it into the fire had been ill-advised.

"We should probably all go outside until the air clears,"

Isabelle said.

"Maybe just *you* should leave," Honey snapped.

Mady looked from Honey to Isabelle and didn't say anything, but she followed Isabelle outside.

Honey looked as though she might stay, to make a point. But she was coughing, too, so she joined them in the fresh air, slamming the door shut behind her.

Loudly, she demanded, "Why would I intentionally pick blister weed?"

"I never said you did," said Isabelle.

Mady looked from one of her daughters to the other. "What happened?" she asked.

At that moment, Frayne came running up to the house from the wheat field where he had been working. "Good news!" he cried. "Most excellent, hopeful news! Webley just came by to say that he and some of the others have been carefully sifting through the rubble and ashes of the witch's house. They insist that there is not a trace of human remains. The witch may have escaped justice, but at least—wherever our newborn baby is—she didn't die in the fire. She may well be alive! *Both* our girls might be alive." Oblivious to the tension in the air, Frayne grabbed hold of Mady's hands—wet and slippery from washing as they were—and tried to dance her around the front yard.

"That *is* good news," Mady said. "Oh, that truly is." For a moment she looked as if she were ready to drop everything and renew the search for the baby.

But then, once more, her attention turned to Honey and Isabelle, and she slid her hands out of her husband's grip.

Sourly, Honey said to her father, "*Both* your girls? Don't you have three? Don't I count?"

Frayne said, "Of course you do, my dear. But you were never in danger." His tone was still light, but he knew better than to try to dance with her.

Practically spitting out her words, Honey asked her father, "If the old witch didn't die in the fire, then how did *this one*"—she jabbed her finger at Isabelle—"escape?"

As unpleasant as it was to be poked at by Honey, as venomous as Honey's tone was, Isabelle knew this was a good question. It was a very good question.

Mady said, "The important thing is—she did."

Frayne had finally realized that the situation was beyond him, and he became silent, looking as though he wished he could slip unnoticed back into the wheat.

Honey said, "*I* think the witch intentionally let her go. First of all, I don't think she's Isabelle—I think she's some creature of darkness that the old witch made. She made her, and she purposefully fashioned her to look like Isabelle, to fool people, to fool us. Second, when the time was right—when she'd stolen our beautiful innocent little baby—then the witch released"—again she spat out the word, and Isabelle counted herself lucky that Honey didn't come right out and actually spit on her—"*this* to work more evil on our family."

What Honey said hit close to fears that had swirled in Isabelle's own heart.

Not a princess, or an animal, or a long-lost daughter. But something created by the witch.

The old biddies she and Willa had met the night before could have been right. Isabelle could be a daughter of a different sort entirely. She could be something the witch had intentionally set loose in the world.

Still, Isabelle fought that knowledge. She said, "That's absurd. What evil?"

Honey said, "For some reason, the old witch wants to take all my parents' children from them. She stole Isabelle six years ago, and the baby two days ago, and now she's sent you to spread poison about me."

Poison? All things considered, that was an ill-chosen word.

"What—" Isabelle started.

But Honey talked over her. She told her parents, "She says I brought blister weed into the house. On purpose. To harm all of you. *Why* would I do that?"

Had Honey intended the flowers for all of them, or just for Isabelle? "I never said—"

Honey got even louder. She grabbed hold of Mady's hand, then Frayne's, so that the three of them were linked, and Isabelle was the outsider. And all the while, Honey said, "I didn't. I don't even think it was blister weed, but if it was—"

Honey caught herself up short with a gasp "—*she* brought it in." She turned on Isabelle and said, "You wicked, wicked thing. You . . . witch spawn."

"How could I have brought it into the house?" Isabelle asked. "I just woke up."

Hadn't she?

She remembered the door slamming, Honey walking in with the flowers, Honey's already-washed arms.

Even if the witch had created her to spread wickedness, this particular wickedness was all Honey's doing.

But Honey told her parents, "She sent me out of the house, demanding milk. And suddenly that sprig of blister weed was in the basket of flowers I'd picked—so that you'd think I picked it."

"That's ridiculous!" Isabelle protested. "*How* could I have gotten it so quickly?"

Honey said, "Witches have their ways."

Mady shook her head. She pulled her own still-wet hands out of Honey's damp grip. "No. Honey. I think it was all a mistake—"

"Or maybe she didn't go and fetch blister weed," Honey said. "Maybe it was just the cow parsnip I gathered. But she's trying to convince you that *I* would try to harm *you*—my own beloved family—when we've stood by each other through so much sorrow and evil that has afflicted us."

"Enough," Mady said. "Both of you."

"She's a changeling," Honey shouted, "a dark creature who's

been left in place of our Isabelle. She's a changeling, and she's turning you against me!"

Mady slapped Honey. "Stop!"

For a moment, Honey was too shocked to respond. Then she buried her face in her hands and wept loudly. "She's made you hate me."

"I don't." Mady put her arm around Honey, "There, there," she murmured.

"It's not true," Isabelle told all of them.

"I know," Mady said, but she continued to hug Honey.

Still, Mady's words caused Honey to wail even louder. She jerked herself away from her mother. "You weren't here when the witch came! That time with you in the forest, the witch just put you to sleep, but she *hurt* me. My limbs felt all on fire, and they twitched and flailed out of my control, and that was so frightening, and I didn't know if it would ever go away. And then she took the baby, making sure I could see—rubbing my face in the fact that I couldn't stop her. You think someone who's that vicious would let the real Isabelle return home? Even if this is Isabelle's body, do you think there's anything of Isabelle left in her? She's a tool of the witch! She's a tool of the devil!"

Isabelle didn't know what to say. There was just enough of substance in Honey's ravings that some of it fluttered on the edge of making sense. She could see how people might come to believe Honey's accusations.

In fact, Honey's wailing and shouting had drawn several of the neighbors out of their homes and into their yards. Others were leaning out their windows or had stopped work in their fields to listen to all this commotion.

If I asked now, Isabelle wondered, *how many would believe me, and how many would believe Honey*?

Willa had said that the two old women last night were looking for someone to complain about. How easy would it be for Honey's accusations to get everyone thinking the same way?

All Isabelle could say was, "The witch didn't send me."

And she wasn't even sure that was right.

"Do you really *know* that?" Honey demanded. "Has your fickle memory suddenly come back so that now you know that?"

"I know I'm not trying to hurt anyone," Isabelle said. "I know I'm not the one who brought blister weed into the house, then tried to get *you* to touch it."

"Well, neither did I!" Honey wailed. "Stop trying to blame me for everything!"

"You're the one—"

Mady interrupted, "Honey, calm yourself. You're going to make yourself ill." By now, she too had noticed the neighbors, and her back had stiffened in embarrassment. "The smoke must be gone by now," she said, and she opened the door. Eager to get away from the neighbors' curiosity, she led Honey indoors.

Still outside on the stoop, Isabelle heard Mady say, "Why don't you lie down for a while? Isabelle, fetch a wet cloth—"

"No!" Honey shrieked. "Don't let her touch me! Don't let her near me!"

"Hush," Mady said. But she also said, "Frayne, could you . . ."

Frayne, who had been unable to decide what to do and had taken only one hesitant step into the house, now hesitated, glancing back at Isabelle.

She warned him, "Not the cloth we were using to scrub our arms with. That one may have blister weed sap on it. Better get a fresh one."

For someone who sounded so close to hysteria, Honey seemed quite able to follow the conversation from both inside and outside the house. "If she wants you to use a specific cloth, that must mean she's done something to it!" she shouted.

"No," Isabelle said, "it's just . . . just in case . . ."

"Take one from the middle of the pile," Mady instructed Frayne. She sounded exasperated with Honey. If she had asked Isabelle's opinion, Isabelle would have suggested another slap or two might be just what Honey needed.

Frayne looked apologetic as he stepped around Isabelle and went further into the house.

Honey managed to kick the door closed behind him.

Isabelle didn't want to go back in.

There hadn't been that much blister weed, and with the

shutters open, the smoke had already dissipated. But the poison Honey was spewing showed no sign of lessening.

Still, if Isabelle left, Honey eventually had to calm down. Her accusations wouldn't have such weight without that sobbing, close-to-retching intensity.

Isabelle opened the door and said, "Maybe I should move into Auntie's house—"

Honey cried, "And turn her against all of us!"

A look of panic shot across Mady's face. She said, "Maybe it would be best if you went to Edyth's house, just for a little while. Willa will cheer you up."

Isabelle's impression of Mady had certainly softened—but obviously the great-aunt's wealth was still something that Mady would take no chance of losing.

And, as for Edyth's house, Isabelle and Willa had never made it that far last night. "I don't know where it is," she said. "I'll go visit Avis instead."

Mady, who'd been sitting on the edge of Honey's bed, started to stand, perhaps to accompany Isabelle; but Honey grabbed hold of her hand and wailed, "Don't leave me when I need you, Mama!"

Mady wavered. Then she asked Isabelle, "Do you feel fit enough for the walk?"

Isabelle wanted to say *no*. She wanted to say, *I need you, too.*

But she didn't force Mady to choose between them. Instead, Isabelle nodded to indicate she was well enough.

Mady sat back down again.

Without clear direction from his wife, Frayne—wetting down a buff-colored piece of cloth—gave Isabelle a halfhearted wave with his free hand.

Call me back, she mentally wished at them. *Tell me to stay. Reassure me that I am not an evil creature formed by the witch.*

But they didn't.

She gently closed the door behind her.

CHAPTER 12

Isabelle knew that it was shorter to cut through the forest than to go around the cluster of village houses and the outlying farms. Her leg was feeling much better, but there was no point in walking more than she had to.

The woods were not spooky and desolate. There was a stream, which helped her determine which direction she was traveling in, and there appeared to be quite a few paths—probably shortcuts from one farm to another.

She went down to the streambed to kneel beside it and splash cold water on her face.

A shred of color by the water's edge caught her attention. She would have ignored it—the woods were bright with flowers and flowering bushes and flitting birds—but something tugged at her memory.

So few things did that.

After cooling down her face, she stood and walked closer. It was a tatter of cloth. Russet. The color of foxes, but also the color of a certain blanket that had been reworked into a rug and a cap. And at least one other fragment had ended up in the pile of rags. This appeared to be a rag also, for the piece was worn, with the edge frayed as though it had ended in a hole.

The cloth was in the water, but it had caught on some stones at the edge, well within Isabelle's reach. Isabelle didn't reach for it, but watched one edge flutter in the mild current.

She was confident of the direction to Avis's cottage, but she needed to settle something in her mind first. Instead of taking the path, she followed the stream, knowing she couldn't get too far lost since she could always follow it back to Mady and Frayne's house.

Isabelle walked at a leisurely pace so as not to put undue stress on her leg. Along the way, she saw daisies, lady's-mantle, angelica—many of the flowers Honey had gathered. Then, rounding a curve in the stream, she saw a tall bush with clusters of white flowers. The individual blooms might look like cow parsnip, but its size showed the plant was definitely blister weed.

Honey had planned it all. She must have known this bush was here, to have been able to find it in the early hours of dawn when the sun would not be beating down, making the sap so dangerous. Even so, Honey had brought a rag to protect the skin of her palm while she broke a piece off. Honey had dropped the blister weed into the basket for Isabelle to touch and the rag into the stream. No doubt Honey had assumed the current would carry the rag away. Then she had washed her hands and arms lest she had accidentally brushed against the plant. Isabelle remembered how she had smelled that morning and how Honey had even thought to bring soap with her when she went to pick the flowers.

Isabelle knew all this. But—would anyone believe her?

Willa might. But she was only twelve years old. What could she do?

Avis would believe her, Isabelle decided.

Probably.

She hoped.

At the least, Avis might have some good advice, and she wasn't prone to shouting or to worrying about offending the great-aunt.

Did you know little Isabelle back then? Isabelle would ask her. *Could I still be her after all and not something fashioned by a witch for a witch's purposes?*

Isabelle planned to ask Avis: *Was I the kind of little girl who would torment an old witch until she put a spell on me? Was I the kind of little girl who would chant:*

Old as dirt,
dirty as dirt.
Ugly as sin,
mean as sin.
Don't let the old witch catch you!

But Avis had seemed to have her doubts from the beginning. "Are you sure she's Isabelle?" she had asked. And, "Wasn't Isabelle's hair lighter and straighter?" And she had even said, "You can come back for a visit . . . or to stay longer, should you decide they're mistaken."

Avis had never believed Mady was right.

Avis had never thought she was Isabelle.

So who, or what, did Avis think she was?

Isabelle chose a path that seemed to be heading where she wanted to go, but very quickly it began to curve away from the right direction. She could retrace her steps and try another path, but there was no telling if that would end up meandering off also. Besides, it wasn't as if this path went entirely the wrong way.

The forest was a friendly place. Isabelle liked its smell, and the sounds and glimpses of the various birds, and the butterflies and chipmunks and squirrels, and the variety of trees and bushes and flowers. She remembered Mady saying, "You always loved the woods." She told herself: *Even if the witch stole me away from my mother while we were in the forest, that wouldn't necessarily have changed my feelings for the place.*

She felt that, somewhere, she had happy memories of being here. If the witch used to send her on errands in the woods . . .

Isabelle shied away from the thought that the witch might have sent her to find blister weed—that *that* was how Isabelle had come to recognize it this morning.

She walked slowly, savoring the woods, letting her mind wander. Like one of those butterflies she was seeing, her thoughts refused to settle and stay on any one thing.

The path led out of the woods, and Isabelle found herself just beyond Thornstowe. She could follow the road—the same one she'd ridden on in the cart that Frayne had pulled. But the road looked hot and dusty, and there was the chance she might meet people along the way.

As long as she walked slowly, her leg seemed able to support her. So Isabelle ducked back under the cover of the trees and retraced the path into the woods, then chose another branching.

And then, suddenly, intruding on all those rich forest smells, there was smoke.

No, not exactly smoke. It wasn't that something was burning; something had burned.

Of course something had burned. The old witch's cottage.

Though not, apparently, the old witch herself. Or Mady and Frayne's youngest daughter.

Isabelle felt a shiver of fear.

Frayne had said the villagers had not found the remains of the baby or the witch. If the witch was still alive, could she be somewhere nearby?

No, surely a sensible witch would have fled.

Unless there was something to hold her here.

Something like Isabelle?

Could it be that, while the villagers had been attacking the witch's cottage, the witch had needed to cast another enchantment, to protect herself, to escape? Could this escaping spell have taken all her concentration, and so the Isabelle-binding spell had broken?

But now, two days later, with the villagers back in town, might not the witch be looking for Isabelle?

Surely, the forest was not a safe place to be.

And yet Isabelle did not turn back.

Instead, she followed her nose.

CHAPTER 13

There wasn't much left of the cottage—a few charred boards, a trampled garden. There was nothing left to recognize or not to recognize. Isabelle felt a deep sadness, a sense of loss, but she couldn't tell what she grieved for. Her lost years? Her life as it might have been?

Something rustled in the underbrush.

Fool! Isabelle chided herself. She had ignored her better judgment in coming here, thinking she might learn something—and now she would learn all, for the witch would step out into the clearing and once again turn Isabelle into her slave, if that's what she was, or into an animal if Orsen were right. . . . Why was she thinking of Orsen's absurd speculation again?

Perhaps it was because she was seeing an animal, not a witch after all. It was a goat, peeking out from between the branches of a bush at the edge of the small clearing, a little black and white goat.

Ungracefully, the creature leaped free of the bush and

boldly approached her. It said "baaaa" and butted her with its head.

The poor thing had probably belonged to the witch. It had run away from the shouting, torch-brandishing villagers, and only now felt safe coming out. Isabelle looked and saw that it was a she-goat, but young, not a nanny goat. So it didn't need to be milked. It probably wanted to be fed and watered.

"I'm sorry," Isabelle told the goat. "I have nothing for you."

The goat didn't believe her and tried munching the trailing edge of her sleeve.

"You are not starving," Isabelle told the goat. "You've just become lazy."

"Baaaa," the goat told Isabelle.

Mady kept goats. Maybe she would like an extra one, if this one indeed had been the witch's once and was now ownerless.

Unless, of course, Honey got all fearful about what evil might be done by a goat that had been raised by a witch.

Avis would be more sensible, Isabelle thought. And Avis and her family had been so kind when Isabelle was a nobody, a lost girl with no memory, and not—potentially—a rich great-aunt's favorite.

Isabelle didn't leave right away but walked around the ruins of the house several times, with the goat following her.

"There's nothing here," Isabelle said. Nothing for the goat, nothing for her. Even if anything had survived the fire—and Isabelle had no idea what that might be—the men who had searched would have found it first, for they had been looking for singed scraps of cloth or hair or bits of bone.

What are you hoping to find? she asked herself. She could think of nothing that the cottage might have held that could prove she really was Isabelle.

She sat down abruptly, her dog-injured leg suddenly feeling heavy and wobbly.

The goat circled her, like a cat looking for just the right place to sit. Then it folded its legs beneath itself and lay down by her side.

"We'll rest for a little bit," she told the goat. She rubbed its ear, which was soft. Somehow she'd known it would be soft, and the rest of the animal's fur would be rather bristly. So . . . apparently she knew about goats. She wondered if tending this animal had been one of the duties the witch had set for her.

Honey must have calmed down by now, with or without convincing her parents that Isabelle—raised by a witch—had to be evil. Isabelle suspected Honey would not have convinced Mady—because that would mean the family must give up plans for ever inheriting the great-aunt's house and property. So, Mady probably had come looking for her by now. Mady would have no reason to think Isabelle would have gone to Avis's via the woods, and especially no reason to think she would have veered from the main path. Mady was probably at Avis's house, probably growing anxious that Isabelle wasn't there yet. Probably wondering if Isabelle was gone for another six years.

Still, the sunshine was warm on Isabelle's skin, while a light breeze kept her from getting too warm. After so little sleep the night before, she found herself thinking how pleasant it would be to curl up and take a nap, using the goat as a pillow.

Then she remembered Mady telling about how she had grown sleepy in the woods, and only later realized the witch must have cast a spell on her.

Instantly alert, Isabelle struggled to her feet so quickly she startled the goat.

Perhaps this had been normal fatigue after a sleepless night. Or, even if it were a spell, that didn't mean the witch was nearby or even alive. She may have set up wards to protect her home—but it would be foolhardy to wait here to see.

Isabelle started walking in what she hoped was the direction of Avis's house, and the goat scampered to keep up.

She had not gone far when—finally—she recognized something. Absolute certainty washed over her that she knew this place. A moment later she remembered where she recognized it from. There was the tree she had tried to climb to get away from Browley's dogs, not very far at all from the witch's house.

Isabelle stopped again, her leg aching.

Someone was coming toward her. This time she was sure it was a person, not another goat.

She realized she had been gone so long that this may well be someone coming to look for her. When Mady found out that Isabelle had never reached Avis's house, she and Avis, both, would have come out looking for her.

It isn't necessarily the witch, Isabelle told herself. *It could just as well be Avis or Browley or Mady or Frayne.*

But the person coming toward her was, in fact, Honey.

CHAPTER 14

Isabelle took a close look to make sure Honey wasn't carrying any blister weed. Or stinging nettles, poisonous toadstools, or snakes.

"I'm sorry," Honey said all in a rush. "I don't know what I was thinking. Mother talked sense into me. I realize I accused you unjustly, that you couldn't have brought blister weed into the house. It must have been me—if you're convinced that's what it genuinely was—but I truly didn't do it intentionally. I must just not have been paying attention."

"I see," Isabelle said. She didn't believe a word of it. But she wasn't going to accuse Honey of being a liar who was out to cause her injury. Or to murder her. Or, failing that, to turn everyone against her. There would come a better time to confront Honey—not when they were alone in the woods together, with only a small she-goat for protection.

"We went to Avis's house so I could apologize, but you weren't there, and Mother became so worried she nearly went into a frenzy."

"Well then," Isabelle said, "I should hurry there to set her fears to rest." She took a half step forward, hoping Honey would move out of her way, but Honey stood planted where she was.

Isabelle evaluated the likelihood that she could knock Honey down—not very likely at all, since Honey was five or six years older and quite a bit bulkier. As for Isabelle's being able to outrun her, that seemed even more impossible, given that she couldn't remember the forest and that her leg was on the verge of giving out.

Honey said, "There won't be anybody there. Avis told Mother you'd probably taken the road, but that you must have tired and stopped at one of the houses. So they're heading back that way, stopping to knock at every door to see if that's what happened, Mother on one side of the road, Avis on the other. If Mother makes it all the way home without finding you . . ." Honey shook her head. "She'd assume the worst. After all she's been through, that would be the end of her."

Everything Honey said was reasonable. It was very similar to Isabelle's own earlier reflections.

This didn't make Honey appear any less lethal.

If I can't escape her, Isabelle thought, *can I get her to go away*? She said, "I'll go back home, and you run ahead until you get to where they are and tell them all is well."

"Isabelle," Honey said, "do I look like the kind of person who's good at running?"

It was pointless. Obviously, Honey was here for a reason, and that didn't bode well. Still, Isabelle said, "Or we could both wait at Avis's house"—not that she relished that idea—"and send Ravyn ahead."

Honey shook her head. "Avis didn't want to leave Ravyn home alone, so she took her along with her. The best thing we can do—and it will be the shortest way, too—is to return home by cutting through the woods. You must have gotten lost on the way here, because it really isn't that far."

Yes, Isabelle thought. *I got lost just enough to see exactly what you were up to with the blister-weed bush.* Naturally, she didn't say that.

Honey finished, "And we're likely to meet Father along the way, because he entered the woods near our house. Once we join up with him, he can carry you."

Isabelle thought there was a hint of resentment in Honey's tone but couldn't be certain. It was often hard to tell what was going on in Honey's head.

Except, of course, when Isabelle suspected she knew *exactly* what was going on in Honey's head.

The goat, having given up on expecting food from Isabelle, butted Honey's hip.

"Shoo. Go!" Honey slapped the goat's rump.

The goat ran a few steps, then stopped to look indignantly at the two girls.

Honey moved as though to take Isabelle's arm.

"I'll be fine on my own," Isabelle said, and Honey accepted this and simply fell into step beside her. The goat, evidently still hoping that food might be coming, followed.

There's nothing I can do for the moment, Isabelle thought. *I can't run away from her; I don't dare let her suspect I don't trust her. What I need to do is bide my time and look out for an opportunity.*

It would have been nice, however, to know what sort of opportunity she was looking out for.

When they got to the burned cottage, Honey asked, "Did you remember anything, seeing this?"

"No," Isabelle said, having no idea if that was the right answer—or if there *was* a right answer.

They walked in silence until the path branched. Isabelle started for the right-hand path, which was the way she had taken to get there, but Honey said, "This way is shorter."

Isabelle considered. She had followed the stream, and then she had taken the path that had ended at the outskirts of Thornstowe. The way Honey was showing seemed as though it *might* be more direct. She glanced at the goat for guidance, but the creature had gotten distracted by a clump of wild strawberries and wasn't even looking at her.

Isabelle followed Honey. The goat eventually caught up, which Isabelle tried to take as a good sign. Not that it made sense to trust a goat about whether a forest route was dangerous or not. Especially when the most dangerous thing about the forest probably was the company she was keeping.

"Are you sure this is the right way?" Isabelle asked, because they were walking up a considerable slope.

"Don't you trust me?" Honey asked with a smirk.

This is it, Isabelle thought. *This is where she makes her move.*

But Honey kept walking. Apparently never expecting an answer, she said, "You must have noticed the stream when you first entered the forest. It passes close to where our yard backs onto the woods."

The stream would have been impossible to miss. Did Honey guess that Isabelle had found both the russet-colored rag and the blister-weed bush by its banks?

Even if Honey had, she didn't appear to be trying to gauge Isabelle's reaction. She nodded toward the lower ground to their right, and Isabelle saw the stream. "It's drier up here," Honey said. "Less overgrown. And we're less likely to sink up to our knees in mud."

There *had* been boggy patches.

"Does any of this look familiar?" Honey asked.

Isabelle shook her head. "Why? Did we like to play here together?"

She could guess the answer by the expression on Honey's face even before Honey spoke.

"Not especially. You had Willa to play with. Besides, you were six. I was almost twelve. That's the same as expecting you and Ravyn to play together."

"I like Ravyn," Isabelle protested.

The polite thing for Honey to answer was that she'd liked Isabelle. But all she said was, "You wouldn't want to play with her day after day. Mother was *always* saddling me with you. I don't understand people wanting a whole packload of children, just so the older ones can take care of the younger ones. I don't ever want to have children."

Isabelle bit her tongue to keep from saying, *Probably all for the best.*

Honey said, "Avis isn't her true mother, you know."

It took a moment for Isabelle to follow the jump Honey had made from herself and Mady to Ravyn and Avis. "I never thought she was," Isabelle said finally.

Honey added, "Nor grandmother, either. Avis and Browley took her in when she was a tiny baby. She's no kin to them at all. They took her in from some people who were just passing through, people who were too poor to keep her."

How sad, Isabelle thought.

Honey said, "I have to remind her of that sometimes, when she gets sassy or pert, that her own parents gave her away when she was but a tiny baby."

"How generous of you," Isabelle said, "to take that responsibility on yourself."

Honey snorted. "But the reason I asked whether you know the area is because this is where Mother lost you."

Isabelle welcomed the excuse to stop walking, because she didn't want to say, *My leg hurts. Please slow down*. "Here?"

Honey gestured vaguely. "Around here somewhere. Mother and Isabelle, out a'berrying. Mother, lazy thing that she is, decided to take a nap, since I wasn't there to hand the child over to. She says falling asleep was part of the witch's spell, but I don't think so. Mother was always prone to naps. Do you want to see the hole?"

"What hole?"

"The one they thought Isabelle might have fallen down, because Browley's dogs kept yipping and yapping by the edge. It's a place where the stream undercut the bluff, so the ground caved in. Here, right by that big tree that's all tipped over from it. Oh, you should have heard Mother when she thought her sweet little Isabelle was at the bottom of that hole. Such a fuss she made."

There was no way Isabelle was going anywhere near the edge of the bluff, though it wasn't that high—only four or five times her own height. Nor would she approach the big tree that marked the hole. She backed away, and Honey followed her.

"Imagine our surprise," Honey said, "when it turned out there was no Isabelle down there. And do you know why there wasn't?" She didn't wait for Isabelle to answer. She said, "Something must have eaten her—because I *know* she was down there."

And, with that, she shot her arm out, shoving against Isabelle's shoulder.

For a second, Isabelle didn't panic. Honey was knocking her down, but they weren't anywhere near the tree.

Except, she realized, that Honey had lied; the hole wasn't by the tree—it was right there behind her.

In the long moment while Isabelle was falling, two things happened.

First, she thought, *Oh. So THAT'S how Honey could be so sure all along that I wasn't her sister.*

Then, in the last instant before she hit the ground, she learned it was true when people said that in times of danger your life flashes before you. Isabelle's life flashed before her.

All of her life.

CHAPTER 15

Images flickered in her mind:

A big town by a seaport . . .

Her parents . . .

Discovering she had abilities that people called magical . . .

Traveling—sometimes in a hurry when those around her grew suspicious or resentful of her abilities, sometimes because she wanted to see more of the world . . .

Growing older . . .

And older . . .

And older yet . . .

The first person who called her the old witch of the forest . . .

Listening to the children taunting her . . .

Mady, that foolish and grasping woman with one daughter whom she ignored and another whom she was grooming to be named heir of the wealthiest woman in the town of Thornstowe . . .

Herself, walking through the woods, looking for plants that could be used in compresses and infusions—since magic is strong, but nature is stronger yet . . .

Spying Mady, asleep under a tree, and the younger daughter, Isabelle, awake and bored and wandering off . . .

The older daughter, Honey, drawing the younger away, away, away . . .

Hearing the little girl's scream . . .

Seeing Honey, kneeling at the edge of the hole that led to the underground caves the stream had eaten out of the bluff . . .

Herself, wondering, Had Honey pushed or simply allowed the little one to fall?

Honey, brushing the dirt from her knees . . .

Honey, leisurely walking away—heading in the direction of her home, not back to her mother, who was closer . . .

The little Isabelle, sprawled at the bottom, not moving, the flowers she'd been gathering spread around her . . .

Herself, climbing down the hole . . .

The child still breathing . . .

Carrying her through the secret ways of the caves and back to the cottage . . .

The distraught parents banging at her door . . .

Determining that Mady was incapable of watching over the child . . .

Determining to keep her safe . . .

Another day, another baby: Mady gone somewhere, Honey left in charge . . .

Seeing Honey carrying the baby into the woods . . .

Herself, running to the caves . . .

Positioning herself . . .

Waiting . . .

Catching the baby safe in her arms . . .

Honey, looking down at the two of them, the look of satisfaction on her face turning to horror at the realization of a witness . . .

The villagers' shouts . . .

Their outrage . . .

Knowing they would never listen . . .

The baby hidden . . .

A too-hasty spell, not well thought out: Change this old body to that of a child . . .

The memories, as well as the years, draining away . . .

Running in the forest . . .

CHAPTER 16

So she wasn't really Isabelle. She wasn't even really a little girl. She was the old witch of the forest.

Almost dying, with her life flashing before her eyes as she fell—or maybe it was when she actually hit the ground—the old witch's spell had disintegrated. But it was not just her memories that had returned—so had her own appearance.

The old witch caught her breath. Was grateful to find she still had a breath to catch. Stirred, and was grateful she could still move.

I really need to stop falling out of trees and down holes, she thought. *I am definitely too old for that.*

She hurt all over, but some parts of her hurt more than others. Worst of all was her right wrist. The hand was floppy and already starting to swell. Unquestionably broken. But there was also a gash running from knee to ankle where a jagged rock had scraped her leg—her previously good right leg—on her way down. Not only did that hurt; it was bleeding. The rest of the cuts and bruises could wait, but that required immediate attention—before the loss of blood made her any more light-headed than she already was.

Gingerly and somewhat squeamishly, the old witch tried to push the two flaps of skin together with her left hand and her throbbing and next-to-useless right. *Stop feeling sorry for yourself,* she thought. *This isn't nearly as bad as what the poor real Isabelle suffered.*

Six years earlier, the little girl had needed much healing.

But that knowledge didn't make the old witch's aches any less real.

She could see there were bits of dirt and grit under the skin she was trying to adjust.

Healing spells work best when accompanied by proper medical technique—such as cleaning out wounds and setting broken bones. Herbal poultices help, too. But there was no time for any of that now.

At this point, it seemed foolish to distinguish between her newer injuries and the partly healed ones from Browley's hunting dogs. The ability to walk quickly and surely would be worth the little bit of extra magic on top of what she needed to move at all.

The old witch rested her head on her knees against the dizziness she knew would follow, and she cast her spell.

The magic burned and skittered through her body.

Like fiery spiders running through my veins, the witch

thought when the sensation had faded enough so that she once again could think. It didn't help that spiders were among her least-favorite animals.

She would pay for this magical shortcut by day's end, when she would be too weak to move and she would need to find a safe place to sleep. It would be a magic-tinged sleep that would last at least a day or two, so it had better be someplace where neither Honey nor irate villagers with torches could find her.

In the meantime, she needed to go out into the world. And for this she felt that, despite Honey's desire to kill her, generally speaking she would be safer if she continued to look like the little girl who people—well, at least some people—thought might be Isabelle, rather than like her old self. *Everybody* was out to get the old witch; only Honey was out to get Isabelle.

The witch waited for the light-headedness of the healing spell to pass, determined not to make the same mistake as before.

This time she cast a spell to make herself *look like* a twelve-year-old girl, not to be a twelve-year-old girl. That meant that—along with her memories—she still had the aches and pains of her old-witch body, but those were familiar.

The old witch stood. With the dog bite and tree scrapes finally healed, it was good not to feel wobbly—well, no more wobbly than was natural from standing on this pile of rocks.

Still, climbing up the sheer sides of the hole she had fallen into would be beyond her. Young or old, injured or healthy, anyone shorter than ten feet tall would need a rope.

But up was not the only way out. What was not obvious from forest level was that this hole was not self-contained, nor was it one of a kind. Eons ago, when the waterway had been more river than stream, it had eaten a series of interconnected caves into the foot of the bluff. Then the water had lessened and withdrawn, leaving the caves dry. Eventually, the ground above had collapsed, opening this one chamber to the sky. Over the generations, some adventurous souls had explored, but none as thoroughly as the witch, who always liked to be aware of multiple possibilities for escape and hiding. She had chosen to move to Thornstowe precisely because of the caves, and she knew all the secret ways through the underground tunnels.

Now she cast the spell to give light to see by, because she hated the dark. A witch never needed to get used to the dark or to worry about candles. She could leave a magical glow burning all night long—a handy thing for someone who was always at least half expecting provoked villagers to burst in.

The way she took led to the cave beneath her cottage, but the trapdoor which should have opened up beneath her kitchen table was stuck. She could lift it perhaps the span of two fingers but no more and thought, too late, of the weight of the collapsed cottage.

Foolish! she chided herself. She would have to take another of the routes to get out, one that would lead farther away.

But then she heard a sound. Someone walking? Someone pushing something out of the way?

The trapdoor lifted, letting in daylight. And there was Avis, peering down at her.

"Well," Avis said, "this is a surprise."

Her tone was friendly, and it was this that reminded the witch that—despite what she knew herself—to everyone else she would appear to be a twelve-year-old girl, the twelve-year-old girl Avis and her family had taken in.

The witch heard Ravyn's voice: "What kind of surprise? A good surprise or a bad surprise? Is it something scary? Is it something I shouldn't see? You don't sound scared, so it must be a good surprise."

Before Avis had a chance to answer any of these questions, Ravyn had wriggled herself into the space between her grandmother's arm and the open trapdoor.

"Isabelle!" Ravyn squealed, and she moved forward, ready to climb right down into the underground hole with the old witch, who was as delighted to see Ravyn as Ravyn obviously was to see her.

It was only Avis catching hold of the back of her dress that kept Ravyn out. "Let her climb up," Avis told her granddaughter, "rather than you climb down."

Ravyn could stand still—briefly—but she couldn't stop talking. "I've named Hercules Turnip's puppies. Do you want to hear their names? They're perfect names. The littlest one, do you remember, the one with the black spot around his nose—"

"Not now, Ravyn," Avis said.

"—the pup Orsen said was a runt, only he's not—"

"Ravyn . . ."

"—that one is Ursa Minor, like the constellation, because that spot on his nose looks like a star, and Ursa means 'bear' and I want Ursa Minor to think of himself as big and strong like a bear"—she lowered her voice as though to keep the pup from hearing—"but Minor, because—really—he is tiny. And the little girl dog? I—"

Avis moved her hand from the back of Ravyn's dress to over her mouth. "Ravyn. Hush! Give the poor child a chance to get up out of that hole."

The old witch was having trouble convincing her body to move as a child would.

Avis reached down to give her a hand up.

With her grandmother's hands occupied, Ravyn's mouth was once more in working order. She asked, "What were you doing down there? Were you exploring? Were you looking for your missing baby sister? Did you find her? Did you know puppies' eyes don't open right away? But babies' eyes do open right away, so if your sister was down there, she wouldn't be happy because of the dark. Did you listen for crying?"

It was fortunate that they still thought she was Isabelle, though pretending she was when she herself no longer believed it might prove difficult. For now, finally out of the hole, the witch said, "I thought the two of you were helping Mady look for me along the road." She wondered if she had lost time at the bottom of the hole. "Are you finished so soon?"

"No," Avis said. "Mady went with Frayne, not us."

Another of Honey's lies.

Why did she believe anything that girl said?

Ravyn added, "We were home when the old witch's goat came, and it kept bleating and knocking its hooves against the wall and butting its head against the door. I told Grandmother it wanted to tell us something. And it did. It wanted to tell us you were under the old witch's cottage, looking for your sister. How did you get under there, with all that stuff on top?"

The witch was relieved to see the young black and white she-goat in the clearing, just beyond. Apparently it didn't like the smell of the burned cottage and would come no nearer. But it bleated "baaaa," as though it recognized they were talking about it.

Avis had put her hand on Ravyn's head, but the witch doubted that would be enough to keep the child quiet. Then Avis said to Ravyn, "Why don't you go see if the goat is all right? It seems frightened to come closer. You go over there, and we'll join you in a moment."

"Do you think the goat has a name?" Ravyn asked. "If not, I can think of one." But she did as her grandmother had told her, leaving the witch alone with Avis.

Avis tipped her head and scrutinized the old witch's face. "It's you, isn't it?" she asked, and the witch knew that—despite the magically youthful appearance of what Avis saw—she didn't mean Isabelle.

"Yes," the witch admitted. Then she told Avis more than she had told her six years ago. She said, "Honey is a murderous young woman, just as she was a murderous young child."

Avis asked, "What are you going to do?"

"Ah," the old witch said. "I have just the plan for that. Are you willing to trust me?"

"Haven't I always?" Avis asked.

CHAPTER 17

The old witch went back to the house that for a brief while—when she'd been Isabelle—she had hoped was hers.

Though she had not been particularly happy to be part of Mady and Frayne's family, now she found herself sad to see the house and to *know* that she didn't belong there. Her true family was long, long gone. No one was left in the world who remembered her as a child, who had grown up knowing the same people, seeing the same things, hearing the same stories. Avis had been a good neighbor for as long as the witch had lived on the outskirts of Thornstowe, but that wasn't the same. It made the old witch feel slightly faint to realize how alone she was, or maybe that was just the effect of having cast the healing spell on herself.

She listened by the window, since she wasn't tall enough to see in.

No voices.

That might mean everyone was still out searching for her.

Or, it might simply mean that no one was talking.

But Honey was almost assuredly home. Mady and Frayne probably told her to stay here just in case Isabelle returned. But Honey would know that wasn't going to happen. She thought she had killed the real Isabelle six years ago.

And now she'd think that she'd just rid herself of a second girl, the girl Honey *knew* wasn't her sister, regardless of what the rest of her family had believed. So Honey would have rushed directly back here. That way, when the body was discovered, Honey would say she had remained behind all the while, in the hope of good news.

The witch didn't dare delay long enough to make sure Honey was alone. She opened the door just a crack and peeked in.

Honey was sitting on her parents' bed—shoes and all, which was a fairly good indication Mady and Frayne weren't home. Another hint was that Honey was eating the last of the sweet cake Mady had prepared the evening before.

As the witch looked on, Honey picked up Mady's mirror, the one with the cunningly carved tortoise handle. Honey gazed into the glass, and her eyes filled with tears.

Guilt after all? the old witch wondered.

Honey spoke, her voice quavering: "She's dead? She can't be. She . . . she just yesterday was restored to us." Honey's chin quivered, and she brought her hand up to cover her mouth, to stifle a moan.

Oh, the witch realized. *Practicing*.

Honey noticed a crumb on her chin and popped that into her mouth. Distracted from rehearsing her reaction to hearing about her just-restored-sister's death, she picked up the ornate comb and ran it through her hair.

The witch remembered the talk from the previous evening about Mady combing Isabelle's hair. She had probably combed both girls' hair, when Honey had been younger, so there was no reason for Honey to have felt left out.

Unless, of course, Auntie had given Mady the elaborate comb after Isabelle had been born, when Honey would have been too old to have her mother comb her hair.

Even so, the witch thought: *Honey tried to kill her sister Isabelle six years ago, tried to kill her baby sister two days ago, set the villagers on me for fear I'd tell that I'd seen her drop that newborn down the hole, and tried to kill the little impostor girl she thought I was.*

And now here she is grooming herself and snacking.

That went a great way toward stifling any sympathy the witch might have felt toward her.

Still looking like that little impostor-Isabelle girl, the witch opened the door, and Honey immediately dropped the comb and mirror and tried to brush the crumbs off the blanket.

But only for a moment.

"You!" she gasped. "Who *are* you?"

"I'm the old witch. And I thought you should know that—

despite your worst intentions—both of your sisters are safe." Then, because she wasn't cruel—even though she was a witch—she added, "As I hope you will be."

With that, she used the same spell on Honey that she had used on herself—except more so. In the time it would have taken Ravyn to say "Hercules Turnip" three times, Honey's features melted from those of a young woman, to an adolescent, to a child, to a toddling babe, to a newborn.

The old witch was unsympathetic, but not heartless. She rushed forward to keep the infant from falling off the edge of the bed since Honey was now too young to sit up on her own. At barely a month old, she was so young she could scarcely hold her head up.

But there were two advantages to this: One, the witch hoped to use baby Honey to replace Mady and Frayne's just-lost baby, the one the old witch really *had* taken. And two, at this age Honey was too young to be confused or to miss her memories. She would never be able to piece things together the way the old witch herself had.

So, the witch thought, *now Mady will get a second chance to raise Honey*.

The witch could only trust that this wasn't folly, that Mady had learned things about mothering and that—as an only child—Honey would fare better this time. Maybe without her bitter memories, she might turn out better, too.

Honey's clothes had shrunk right along with her. Most babies do not wear dresses with cinched-in waists and bodices meant to show bosoms at their best advantage. The dress not only looked silly, it would be recognized as a miniature version of what Honey had been wearing the last time she had been seen. All a baby this small needed was a blanket, and for that a soft piece of rag from the rag pile would do. As for the grown-up clothes, the witch tossed those into the hearth, adding a dollop of magic to make sure the fabric burned completely.

Even that tiny bit of enchantment made the witch sway as weakness crept into her bones. What with the healing spell and the spell to keep her looking like the Isabelle whom Avis and Ravyn expected to see, and the spell that had turned Honey into a baby, the witch's energy was fading. She had to hurry, or she would collapse before she got back to the burned cottage where she'd asked Avis to wait for her.

Baby Honey stirred and fretted in the witch's arms. The witch tried jostling her as she walked back to where her cottage had once stood, but all that did was bring on hiccups. Baby Honey announced their arrival by beginning to cry.

"Isabelle! Isabelle!" Ravyn cried. "You *did* find the baby! Where was she? Was she underground? Did you have to fight the old witch for her? Did she have a spell on her? Were there any other children down there?"

"Hush, Ravyn," Avis said, but mostly she was occupied with making faces for the baby and tickling the baby's soft little belly and wiggling her fingers in the babe's tiny face.

"Ravyn," the old witch said. "I wish I could answer you, but I cannot."

"Why can't you?" Ravyn asked. "Did the witch put a spell on you so that you can't say? If I guess, will the spell permit you to say yes or no? Blink once for yes, and twice for no. Does—"

"Ravyn!" the witch and Avis exclaimed simultaneously.

"What?"

The witch said, "There is no spell. But I need you to run and find Mady and Frayne to tell them that your grandmother has the baby."

"*You* have the baby," Ravyn pointed out.

The witch handed baby Honey to Avis.

Avis, who had more experience with babies than the witch did, rocked baby Honey and cooed gentle sounds to her.

"All right," Ravyn said. "Now I can tell them."

She spun around to run with her news, but the old witch called her back, even though there was no time to spare: "Ravyn!"

"What?" Ravyn asked.

The witch kissed the top of her head, even though she knew this was an unlikely gesture from the twelve-year-old she appeared to be.

"What's that for?" Ravyn asked.

"Because I wanted to," the witch told her.

Ravyn hugged her. "And I wanted to do that. Shall I fetch Mady and Frayne now?"

"Yes, please."

As soon as Ravyn was out of sight, the old witch said to Avis, "Please tell Mady and Frayne that Honey and I rescued the baby, and that the two of us are now off to seek our fortunes."

Avis made a skeptical face that reminded the witch of the kind of face Orsen would make. "I don't see how they could ever believe that," Avis said.

"Here's the baby—well, *a* baby, anyway—and no sign of the two of us, so I don't know what else they *can* believe. And please tell the great-aunt that old people have to be on their best behavior or nobody comes to visit them. And tell Browley thank you for rescuing me from his dogs that were supposed to be tracking the old witch. And tell Ravyn to be happy. Especially tell Ravyn to be happy. And not to spoil Hercules Turnip's puppies."

Avis nodded. "I can do all that." She gave the old witch a one-armed hug, because baby Honey had fallen asleep and Avis didn't want to disturb her. "Thank you," she said. "For everything." She bit her lip. "I never asked you before . . ." She hesitated. "When, six years ago, you brought Ravyn to me, I never guessed . . . But seeing that you can change people's ages . . ."

"Don't ask now," the old witch said.

Like Honey, Ravyn had been bespelled to an age younger than memories. She would never remember that she was once a little girl named Isabelle whose mother had tried to groom her to be her great-aunt's favorite and whose sister had tried to kill her. Even if people had thought it was odd that a six-year-old girl had disappeared the same day that some strangers nobody but Avis had seen had abandoned a tiny baby—even so, nobody could ever put the two things together.

Because Browley had been kind, the old witch advised, "Leave your husband thinking it was wandering strangers, not me. It would only distress him, seeing as he believes in witches."

Avis smiled. "*Will* you be leaving?" she asked. "Or just changing to yet another age?"

It was tempting. Avis, Browley, and Ravyn were as close to a family as the witch had had in a long, long time. But it would never work.

"Thornstowe can stand just so many strangers bearing babies," the witch said. "It's past time I move on. Good fortune to you and your family."

Avis grinned knowingly and said, "And to you and yours."

The witch nodded gratefully. Her limbs felt heavy and hard to move, and this time she was definitely getting light-headed from the effect of all the magic she had done. She told herself it was her fatigue that was making her already miss being Isabelle, but she suspected there was more to it than that.

She needed Avis's help to go back down through the trapdoor, taking the black and white goat with her. Not liking the smell of the burned-out cottage or the confines of the tunnel, the little goat balked and bleated, though it grew calmer once Avis closed the door above them so that it could no longer see a way out. And it seemed to like the glow the old witch held in her hand.

As the old witch led the goat down the tunnel, she could hear Avis move debris back over the trapdoor.

The witch let the appearance of Isabelle go, in an effort to stop the waning of her strength.

It helped, but not much.

She told the goat, "We should be safe in the caves, because nobody else comes down here. I can sleep and regather my strength; and when we're in a safe place, I'll change you back into a baby, but—really—you're better off as a goat for now." *Anything* was better off than being Honey's sister.

The old witch found a nice cozy dry spot for them to rest in. As the weariness washed over her, she wondered if Ravyn had come up with a name for the goat, and she decided that, yes, Ravyn almost certainly would have.

"You're lucky," she told Mady's month-old baby, "she didn't have a chance to tell me. Your name can wait a little longer until I come up with something on my own."

But for herself, she decided that in her new life she would go by the name of Isabelle.

VIVIAN VANDE VELDE lives in Rochester, New York, with her husband. After publishing her first novel, *A Hidden Magic*, she went on to publish more than forty books, most of them in the genres of science fiction and fantasy. Excerpts from the reviews of her two other books follow:

"Fans of fantasy and horror will relish this tale of suspense and the supernatural."
—*Bulletin of the Center for Children's Books*

"Readers will enjoy Vande Velde's clear prose and vivid imagery along with a hearty dose of suspense."—*VOYA (Voice of Youth Advocates)*

★ "A strongly focused narrative with appeal for middle-grade ghost-story lovers."
—*Bulletin of the Center for Children's Books*, starred review

"Cliff-hanging chapters, engaging characters, and a truly scary first-rate thriller for youngsters." —*Booklist*

Made in the USA
San Bernardino, CA
26 January 2014